FACELESS IN NIPPON

Dale Brett

Expat Press
New York & Miami

Printed in the United States Of America

Excerpts of this manuscript have appeared in different versions online in Back Patio Press, Burning House Press, Detritus Online, Expat Press, Misery Tourism, Muskeg Magazine, RIC Journal and Silent Auctions.

Cover Art and Book Design by Arturo Herman Medrano

Faceless in Nippon is perhaps the most sincere contemporary novel about banality, modernity and existential ennui to exist, this side of 202X. With surprising ease and admirable restraint, Brett competently weaves the tale of one individual's attempt at self-discovery and extreme escape. It is powerful, mildly depressing at times, almost always funny, rarely cynical and completely unironic. I wholeheartedly applaud any writer capable of crafting a complex (but easy-to-follow) story structure without the employ of meta-narratives and post-*everything* tropes. Brett presents a writing style that is both exuberant and attentive—enough, to present juxtapositions that alone, pretty much approach silent excellence and supreme intellectual sophistication. The not-so-subtle anti-groupthink motifs within the text posit a very important question vis-à-vis the perceived status quo, and what is to be expected of humanity, as a whole, in the years to come. There are several breathtaking moments and unique descriptors, like: ambient observations RE: the different colours of the sky, the muted magnificence of neon lights and their effect on the substance of the night, abstract ideas of the ethereal and its ineffable properties, the magickal aspects of vapourwave music, the stunning ethnographical discourse and of course, *Blade Runner*. If any or all of this sounds familiar, I assure you, Brett takes what you think you know, and turns it into the unfamiliar.

—Mike Kleine, author of *Kanley Stubrick* and *Lonely Men Club*

The time has come ... pick up ... put down those bread knives ... Dale Brett has written with a livid expression ... attacking the aluminium fascia of literature ... kicking the coffee cans of Asia. Dale Brett wrote a book. A meditative trance of a novel ... full of nocturnal sounds ... painful blows ... the menial tasks of modern society ... the strange feeling from a variety show ... the bitter taste of cheap drinks ... cup noodles ... late-night advertisements ... J-pop ... and beautiful human bodies. The broken murmurs of inner loneliness ... the blank mass of social media pleasure-feeds ... the convenience store. *Faceless in Nippon*. F.I.N. Fin. Begin. Finnegan's Wake. The beautiful skins of previous worlds. Apartment buildings full of hentai magazines. Glass containers of bizarre taxidermist creatures. Dale Brett's novel isn't some mandatory script ... it is a mental scab ... a burnt-out body encompassing kawaii and key chains ... the public intimacy show ... excessive mayonnaise ... Styrofoam and corporate entrails ... warm waves of gaudy sashes and electricity. Nameless in Japan. Eyeless in Gaza. The overhead ramps of your social conditions. Turbo jets inside a fancy shell. Wasteful conglomerations of real people. This book contains the night's forgotten moments ... the hard times ... the artificial light ... dirty river ... facial expressions ... Japan ... flip phone ... capitalist perfection. Inside ... on these pages ... the glossy lustre of Jesus ... aluminium fascia ... cigarette ash ... greasy convenience store debris. Don't be a suspicious customer ... read this.

—Shane Jesse Christmass, author of *Belfie Hell* and *Xerox Over Manhattan*

CONTENTS

"The arcade is a street of lascivious commerce only; it is wholly adapted to arousing desires. Because in this street the juices slow to a standstill, the commodity proliferates along the margins and enters into fantastic combinations, like the tissue in tumours. – The flaneur sabotages the traffic. Moreover, he is no buyer. He is the merchandise."

– Walter Benjamin

REASONS

* * * * *

Here I am. Walking down the street. Kicking a can. A coffee can. Yeah, that's right. You heard correct. A coffee can. Asia, they love coffee cans. This one has an image of the Boss. Boss fucking coffee. Like in the advertisements. In these commercials, the Boss's face is highlighted with a glossy lustre, his beard and pipe are luminous, the people holding the can radiate with light, they are filled with fucking joy. He is vending machine Jesus. The image of the Boss's face on the can I am kicking is a stark contrast to the one in the commercial. This Boss has travelled a long way. He has taken the hard road. He has paid for his sins. His face has been caved in. His ordinarily well-sculpted beard is a slog of zigs and zags. His iconic pipe is protruding at an odd angle, the glint of the aluminium fascia that houses his image masked by cigarette ash and the remnants of greasy convenience store debris – lost treasures of last night's forgotten moments. This Boss has fallen on hard times. Chalk one up to the tally. We've got ourselves another victim of the streets. If I squint carefully, straining my already depleted eyes, I think I might be able to see my reflection in the blunted surface of the can. Looking closer, squeezing tighter, my eyes burning, the vision of what I think is myself becomes obscured. But it is just a trick of the artificial light. There is nothing staring back at me.

Why am I here? What made me pack up these hot little bags and leave? Well, reasons. Reasons that are not always entirely clear to me. Reasons I'm sure that are there, though. Residing present somewhere inside me, hiding in a deep pit of despair. Wallowing like the irises in a squalid possum's dormant eyes. Reasons aside, whatever these nebulous scraping vibrations inside me are, it became clear that I needed to leave the white, middle-class suburbs of the Western world behind. For a holiday. For good. For a little-long while. I didn't know. I was just certain that I didn't want to opt in to the local no-hope population cycle of mortgages, marriages and making babies. Maybe I was just a displaced soul that couldn't find a dream there. Or maybe I could, and I just hadn't realised yet. Maybe I would return and have these things. My defeat utterly massive in its scale. Society: 1 Me: Zero. But that remained to be seen, whether I would turn out to be another one of the local hegemonic non-beings back home, mornings filled with sausage sizzles, dance classes and hardware stores. Not that these experiences sounded entirely bad. It just wasn't anything I could handle right now. Or possibly ever.

For now, I had 'escaped' to live in Asia. A place where I could be more anonymous and non-committal while still maintaining my self-esteem. A place where I could test my nihilism, reduce external expectations and somewhat control my anxiety. Mowing lawns and watching football games on cinema-sized television sets is not for everyone. The suburban dream of Western culture is not for everyone. Reasons for doing things are not for everyone.

Sometimes, you don't need dreams or reasons. It's refreshing to rely on the mammalian, the reptilian, the rhipidistian brain. Sometimes, you just need to escape. You need change. You want to experience what it is to be a lungfish. To respire through gills. To feel the perfusion of air. To lay on the bed of a dirty river and gulp and stare and make contented facial expressions. Or, sometimes you decide to move to Japan. This is what I think as I traipse across town. Responsibility, escape, lungfish, urban Japan. It dawns on me that my 'reasons' have led me to merely move from one consumer-culture to another. This realisation entirely evident in the crushed face of the Boss as he stares up at me, one eye dented beyond recognition.

I remember taking a holiday to Japan when I was frustrated with my pedestrian life in Australia and thought, 'yep, this is it.' Something about the cities in Japan all being so busy yet so silent, like being trapped underwater or encased in the image of a photograph, time spent moving ceaselessly through urban passages like phantoms submerged by the gentle waves of an amniotic mall, day and night. A new circadian rhythm to re-educate my languid brain. I thought my life could be content if all I did was eat pre-packaged bags of edamame and drink giant cans of Asahi under mutely undulating glass skyscrapers. Interchanging endlessly from train to train as I observed the neutral faces of the local inhabitants with no adult responsibility clawing at my inner core.

I look down at my flip phone and see that I am out of credit. Looks like it's time to pay a visit to the Softbank shop I say to the crushed Boss. This is just between me and you, Boss, I say. Maybe out loud. Though I'm pretty confident it wasn't uttered aloud, that it was internal. But it would be humorous if it was out loud, I think. I try again. I say it out loud. For the effect. It doesn't sound as intended. It is not funny. It reverberates around in the unmanned street. It is sad, weak, pathetic. A man, a banished soldier, on the other side of the world, having a one-way conversation with a two-dimensional face on a can. Talk back to me Boss, I demand. I know you're hurting son, but I need you to respond. You with your face pummelled into a cataclysm of unconventional lines. I know you are used to smoothness, to that Godly capitalist perfection. I'm sorry to put you in this position, but this is where we find ourselves. You, annihilated, moving from dusty corner to corner on these tremulous streets. Me essentially doing the same. We are not so different see, you and I, Boss man. We have transcended our artificial images. We have escaped our previous worlds of false promises and fake smiles. We are like titular snakes shedding beautiful skins. I hope the Boss gets it, I think, as we part ways. People like us, we are rare. Rare pedigree, rarer breeds. We have to stick together in this world. It's lonely up on the mountain when you don't give in and submit to conformity.

My phone vibrates, reminding me of my impending credit debacle. I give the Boss one more stern kick. One for the road, I say. I continue walking down the street. I don't look back. There will be others of course. More crumpled spirits like the Boss. After all, this is Asia and they fucking love coffee cans.

QUEUES

* * * * *

When I arrived in Japan, I had to find an apartment. It became apparent I had a lot of shit to set up. I contacted this guy named Damien to help me source an apartment. That was like his job, 'apartment sourcer.' He picked me up in a squat SUV with a piping hot can of Boss coffee in his hand, the eyes of the Boss staring at me like he knew everything. 'In the future, don't kick my brethren,' he silently screamed at me.

None of the shit I needed to set up for my initial run at life in Japan was spectacular. Just rudimentary, bureaucratic business to take care of. Electricity account, gas account, Internet connection, some sort of municipal registration scheme. All of this 'business' meant a lot of lining up. I was lucky I didn't have a job yet. With Damien's help, I became an expert in the myriad queues of Japan. In Japan, they love queues. They love waiting patiently. I think people enjoy the contemplation, the relaxation. It's all very Zen, which I guess, historically makes sense, if culture and geography are anything to go by. This approach always struck me as something admirable. Back home, people would always complain about queues. They would joke about queues. They would bond over their hatred of queues. They would hold impromptu, avid discussions about why they had to wait too long in certain queues – to attend sporting events, to update their driver's licence, to talk to some hopeless broken employee at the bank about their dollar-less account. They could even do a lot of these things online to avoid, or at least minimise, the time they were standing in a queue. But they never did. They probably didn't realise but waiting in queues was their whole life. Well, the waiting and subsequent bitching. Getting irate about shit that didn't matter was all they had. Their modus operandi. Subconsciously, they seemed to revel in it. My approach was always more like the Japanese regarding queues. Just deal with it as it comes. Use the time wisely. Read a book, think a thought, stalk people on social media. Get used to it people, queues are your life.

After setting everything up, Damien took me to his 'office', which is just a desk on the third floor of the building where people pay rent. Cash only, he says. We went to the office to sign my rental agreement and I paid him a bunch of zeroes and ones. In cash of course. The 7-Eleven ATM allows you to use international cards for a maximum withdrawal of 10,000 Yen. 7-Eleven lets foreigners in Japan withdraw a lot of money. The corporation is cool with it, they know they will get it back from the same patrons bleeding it out of their lined pockets when they purchase giant cans of beer, hentai magazines and deep-fried snacks. There is another desk behind Damien's which is reserved for the elderly Japanese lady who owns the building. Yes, apartment buildings are still owned by single, decrepit living people in Japan. I instantly knew she was the owner, because Damien mentioned it in the car, that her eyes would always be fixated on random points in the distance when he swivelled around to apologise for his rudeness or ask her a question. She would just sit in the back there, pottering around, shuffling bits of paper back and forth like a hyper-stimulated mouse. After I moved in, I would never really speak to her. Not that I really could given the language barrier, but I came to like her for her calm, detached demeanour all the same. She exuded a positive aura and after years of banal neutrality, positive energy was what I dearly needed. Hell, even indifferent energy would do.

When I was signing the rental agreement, I noticed these bizarre taxidermist creatures on display above the elderly lady's desk. There was a bird with brilliant plumage in a glass container up on the highest shelf. Kind of like one of those glass bottles used to store model ships. I stopped Damien during his mandatory script about the terms and conditions of our agreement to ask him what this creature was known as when it walked the earth. Damien said he didn't know. He swiveled to ask the elderly lady that owns the building for me.

"Go-kura-ku-chou." She said.

"Ber-doo of para-dai-su" Damien said nodding benignly.

This was my life now. Silent contemplation in queues and taxidermist birds of paradise.

It sounded like heaven.

STREET SAUCE

* * * * *

Hat on, hood on, expectations low, breathe... Let's take a spin around the yard. Images of tattered lanterns, years of forgotten romances, every wide eyed shutter pulled. Sulking adolescent crags jerried out in the station McDonalds smoke enough cigarettes they could be sick. Plaid skirts and exposed knees expunge any infinitesimal shred of self-proclaimed hovering decency. My thunderous senses shudder like the engineered life machines that tremble above. The delicious, succulent sauce on the street has congealed just in time. Yamatoji Rapid. Special Rapid. Special Local. Special rapid local lives and feelings blur past the wobbling yolk of my eye. Searching for a mental scab to itch, the shells of burnt-out bodies sway in line. Kawaii key chains of dazed girls sit delicately suspended in locomotion with the tracks, visibly arrested like the power of the elderly geezers who try to cop a hit of their feels in the shade of the peak hour jam. Strewn deflowered newspapers depicting the daily horoscopes line the Nippon patriarchy's castration. Pathetic attempts at public intimacy show that it's on full fucking display. Crammed dins of convenience after convenience make it clear that the salarymen want to end up anywhere but home. A glimpse of any one of 21 konbini stumbled upon illustrate a diet of deep-fried animal fat, excess mayonnaise and cheap carbonated booze. Images of dirty manga girls gorged on cuticles old enough to be their disenchanted daughters reflected in despondent pools. The will to live buried somewhere in the encrusted yellow corners of those same weary eyes. Salacious slurping of noodles the most common way to climax, no hope these Styrofoam hieroglyphs smeared with corporate entrails are misinformed. Wheat or egg, thick or thin, cold or hot, hard or fast – just tell 'em how it is. If it's a good deal, you can't refuse it. Just make sure to ask 'em to take a photograph of their family before you pay the cost. Note it down, note it all. If a friend tells you "No," just say "No," to it all. Kids, settle in – this is where it begins.

Moonlit passages spell out words in saccharin orange. Tightly coiled egg sacs of garbage promote the residents' unfounded ideology. I slip a turn past an unsavoury belch of bicycles. Front wheels driven to the ground like rusty anchors on the sideroad. Head nods and frothy sips abound. Trepidation of the hosts mired in side glances. The depth of aimless souls slide past like tragic vessels buried at sea. Delicate drunken office hands play at shadows politely as the smoke from Mild Seven tips filter the cavern within. Vending machines four, five and six – our only good friends in the abyss. Crouch down and slide across the abrasive drywall. Fear that eyes never lock eyes. Knowing glances vibe as they intimate my way. Flesh of a grilled squid permeates an aura of desperation. I insert a few clammy coins for refreshment. Pop, whirr and hiss – the magical delivers a tabular beacon of mighty thirst. Crack it open, shake my knee for a taste, stand around out of tune. Time to light up a stick like the other enervated masses. My lengthy chugs and drags in silence eventually win. This convivial shared weltschmerz shows I've found where I belong.

HUDDLED

* * * * *

Things are going well. Things are somewhat settled. So, I try contacting a girl I had a fleeting relationship with when I worked in a Japanese restaurant back home. She was on a working holiday visa. She told other people she thought I was a good man. That I would make a good husband or father. Or something. I remember the opalescent gloss of her eyes. It was hypnotic, like a supernatural glaze covering her essence.

She has invited me to stay with her. I am nervous, but willing. Her apartment is miniscule. It is alien. It is foreign. Everything looks like it is slightly warped. The utensils, the door handles, the mail piled up on the small dining table. It feels like I am at home, in a closet, on a mild dose of acid. I am heavily struck by a foreign metaphorical object that this place is normal to millions, but to me it is not. Words like beautiful, delicate, outrageous replace 'normal'. The futon laid out, dented and moulded by her lived-in impression. The small box of cosmetics impervious to time as it quaintly rests beside her pillow, ready to be utilised for another day, tomorrow. A rogue plastic bag with a spontaneous purchase from Don Quijote made on a random week-day night – maybe she thought she needed something badly, but she probably really didn't. We never do when we think we do. Don't worry, I am the same. I commit exactly the same sins. I want this and more and more and more. I want to devour all of it. Her organised scenery.

Haunted by her eyes. How long they stare. The orbs glistening with a sheen of expectation. It's just, you see, I don't want to have a bad reaction. I lie, say this is nice, try to remain cool. What I really think, what I want to say, is that I burn for this. I haven't felt so in years. Have forgotten the word 'excited', forgotten what it means. After continuing to scan the apartment, her continuing to scan my face for signs of my intentions, I decide to take the elevator downstairs and have a cigarette. The reedy hall on the other side of the partition to her mundane but spectacular abode smells equally as enticing. I don't know how to describe the odour, the atmosphere, but to me, it feels like something fleeting, something temporary – a force that I need, to be someone else in some other city, in a distant country. Please let me go previous world, I am the one you need to forget. You need to fucking let me go.

The elevator ride is unreal. It is only four floors. It is only a standard issue. I am not on drugs. There is nothing interesting here, for most. Just for me. I try to avoid bursting into tears. Not sure whether this bubbling wave is sparked by joy, sadness, melancholy or some other emotion defined by some specific German word with no direct English translation that I cannot accurately describe. Shit is sparkling though. The doors and walls gleam. Electric is the air.

I somehow calmly exit the elevator at the culmination of its descent. I extract a Marlboro Ice Blast from the black and fluorescent blue package and crush the filtration device. Double mint bitches. Blade Runner, I think. The future. What does the future hold? I only smoke menthol cigarettes in Asia. I only want to feel different. I only want an extended holiday from my Self and everything I supposedly stand for. This was the way it was always going to be, before I was even born. So just take me for who I am. Please, I urge her silently from my position at street level.

I return to her apartment and the pheromones have not dissipated yet. We talk for some time. We cannot communicate well. But it is important to note, verbal communication is not always necessary in this world, or the next. Often, I find, it is even better without it. Uttering syllables aloud can lead to confusion. Too many words only result in complication. I wouldn't want it any other way. I've tried both and I know which I prefer.

The kissing stuff starts. Our clothes find a new home next to the cosmetics besides the futon. I am aroused. I thought I would feel invincible, but my mind starts spiralling into an impending doom. I am nervous, it seems.

I need to go to the bathroom, I stammer. No surprise. Calm down, you haven't lost it yet. I sit on the terrestrial seeming toilet and rub. The mirror-world light and fan that ordinarily would be soothing act menacing as I hope to whatever God I don't believe in that I can get it together. That everything will just work. I get it semi, kind of, somewhat close. I decide that I must return before things start seeming 'suspicious.'

We re-commence where I left off and I pray to those same make-believe Gods that I can keep things together for long enough to provide some form of satisfaction. It's always a problem when the condom goes on, to be able to handle the dulled sense of touch in a hyper-nervous state of contagion. I think I manage it. But I can see from her face, that I haven't managed it well. ~7 minutes is about as much as I can bear before I pretend to cum and disengage. I try to make up for this atrocity by using my mouth, but I know it is too late. The sheen is gone, her orbs are dry.

Later that night, past midnight, I quietly hear her leave the apartment. I don't try to stir. I don't ask her what, where or why. I stay perfectly still and pretend to be asleep. When I am certain she is gone, I climb up onto the window sill. I open a giant can of Asahi and sip it. I don't turn on the light. I feel like Scarlett Johansson in Lost in Translation, huddled on the ledge of the apartment window as I overlook this cross-hatched neighbourhood in a land I am not a citizen of. I think of the chords of My Bloody Valentine but don't put any music on. I think of taxis moving smoothly and seamlessly through neon-soaked nights from better days and memories gone by than this. I think Scarlett Johansson-My Bloody Valentine-taxi drivers with white gloves cruising on neon-soaked nights over and over and over again. Interminably. I check the time. It is after 4am. It is after 4am and I know she won't be back. Know she won't return until I am gone tomorrow. And I don't blame her. Like I said, it is always easier without words. Without confrontation. Texts days later take the sting out of the awkwardness. Words on a screen at a later stage play better at innocence. Innocence is what we want. Because who wants to feel an extra slice of guilt?

BLUE REMINDER

* * * * *

They were known as the holy triumvirate. More tight-knit than onion, bell peppers and celery. I've never been to New Orleans, but I hear these vegetables are meant to be dynamite in bed together. In Australia, this is where they would probably talk about frogs in socks, or something. You know, inuendo. You feel me? What I'm talking about are Apps – or A.P.P.S. as my most recent online fuck buddy calls them. Spell the letters out. Make it an acronym for us all. Acronyms unite over abbreviations. Basically, when you arrive, when you settle in, when you gets to talkin' – there are three.

Line. KakaoTalk. WeChat. These are the offerings from corporate entities you need to download and commit your soul too. These vivid, small tiles on ubiquitous screens will consume you. These super-charged bites of software contain the manifesto you need to pledge allegiance lest you want to end up incredibly lonely. Being displaced is acceptable, but displacement without companionship is too much for anyone.

Firstly, there is Line. This is a Japanese app. Wikipedia advises that "Line began as a disaster response" to deal with the 2011 Tohoku earthquake when telecommunication services were down. Now, it is just like many other instant messaging apps designed to keep people from profound loneliness.

There are a couple of ways to play Line. You can approach someone with the whole "Oh, I'm learning Japanese and you want to learn English! We should totally meet and co-learn with each other!" The girl behind the opposing avatar likely won't understand all, or any, of what you are saying, so you may need to insert a few chunks of copy and pasted Hiragana. The reasons for this are twofold. One, to make her understand that you want to meet up if she doesn't understand any of the English you typed. Two, so she will naively think you know more Japanese than you do, surprising her with your nous and earning a pocketful of bonus points in the process – "Wow! Kawaii!"

For the select few recipients whose English level is more 'advanced', you can approach it by suggesting the 'tour of local attractions' method. "Hey, I'm new here. Any interesting sights in the city?" Yes? Okay, well how about we meet up and you can give me the grand old tour. Bingo Bango. Just like that, you've got your pretext.

Lastly, if you really strike out, you may simply get an invite to a random address in Kanji with a few golden letters typed in English. These solicitous offers are to be treated with caution, but in almost all cases, are legitimate. Such adventures are also an excellent way to see some of the more banal 'every-day' niches of the city's outer extremities off the tourist trail. I have had success in each of these methodologies and would 100 percent recommend them to alleviate, albeit temporarily, the pitted stench of anomie.

Secondly, there is KakaoTalk, which is basically the same as Line except the icon is yellow and it is predominately designed for, and used by, Koreans. There are a surprising number of Koreans in Japan. I have found 'Korea towns' to be an excellent way to blow time without exceeding your daily cash allowance. I often go to these places on the train and buy literal mountains of pickles – kimchi garlic, kimchi cabbage, kimchi beans, kimchi everything. I found the probiotic juice from these babies would keep me going for hours. They also gave my apartment a kind of lived-in vibe I found warmed my heart. I would often daydream that the old ladies behind the stalls had taken the time out of their days to make these fermented goods especially for me. I pretended these old women cared for me like a son, that they wanted to give me every opportunity to succeed in life.

You needed to tweak your game for KakaoTalk. You had to brush up on your K-Pop and your K-food and your K-culture. You had to profess your love for weird shit like fried rice sandwiched between melted cheese topped with a kimchi infused soft-boiled egg. You always had to be on the look-out for plastic surgery. You had only truly won when you found a girl who could pull off the extraordinary K-Pop stroke-wink. Imagine someone permanently closing one eye whilst pouting and giving you the peace sign. That's what I'm talking about.

The last app in your arsenal to meet people was WeChat. This is a Chinese-based app owned by some massive company that pretty much does everything you could possibly imagine. It's like Facebook meets Uber meets online banking. Again, like KakaoTalk, using this app I found there was a surprising amount of Chinese people living and residing in Japan. This app has an added feature where you can search for people in your vicinity. Like, it uses the GPS function to access where other users are in relation to your own geographical position. As I said, this is a Chinese app, so any kind of surveillance tool in-built is par for the course. I didn't mind though, any kind of encounter with the panopticon in exchange for meeting people who I could see, smell and touch was a trade-off I was willing to make.

I would use this app in much the same way as I used Line. Just dropping out a few feelers in the 'I just got here, please show me around' mould. I found that most people I met through this app were fixated on brand-name handbags and luxury cars. I think they struck up conversations with me because their preconception of white foreigners was that they were rich and obsessed with consumer products, which I suppose is a fair, not to mention accurate, inference to have. However, upon meeting me, it was clear I did not live up to this preconceived image. My factory-made, sweat-ridden clothes, my lengthy beard, my choice of venues to meet up being the cheapest café opposed to the most expensive Italian restaurant or sky bar – these were all signs that made WeChat users pull the pin on any attempt I made to bond.

Overall, I found that Line worked best, I just had to meet people to add to the app so I could interact with them. The first date I went on was an unmitigated disaster. I learned that often the person on the other side of the phone was merely using Google translate to respond in English. In person though, they were largely silent. I recall sitting there at a cheap café with this girl, her face red with embarrassment as I asked her questions about herself in the simplest English I could think of. I didn't receive a response to any of the questions except for little nods and murmurs. Small grunting sounds a hamster might make like 'ng' and 'ngngngngngng' as she tried to gain some semblance in a rapidly deteriorating situation. We ordered a margherita pizza and she barely ate anything. Being poor and jobless, I did not let that beautiful edible flying disk go to waste. I ate all of it, including the last piece. When I got home, relieved that the whole thing was finally over, the girl messaged me on Line, and with the assistance of whatever translation service she was using typed: "Can't believe you ate last pizza. I must cry now." I said I was sorry, deleted the message history and never spoke to her again. I sat in silence in the dark while warm waves emanating from the split system heating osculated my face. I had to be more careful in the future. It was a blue reminder that I wasn't here to break other people, I was here to break myself.

PAYING THE BILLS

* * * * *

Every second Thursday, the 'slips' would come rolling in. That beautiful clunk as the white-gloved postman deposited news into the metallic mailbox affixed to my heavy-duty apartment door. Japanese postmen always reminded me of the Beastie Boys as they are dressed in the film clip for "Intergalactic," like cosplay nuclear technicians with wannabe hazmat suits emblazoned with gaudy sashes and scout-like badges. They looked more like camp insect collectors opposed to someone you would entrust mail delivery with. All they needed was an oversized net. These guys were delegated domestic duties only and the correspondence I received from the local Japanese postal service were exclusively bills. Electricity, gas, internet... The necessary services I set up when I met Damien, that was about the extent of it. I really enjoyed it when the 'slips' came rolling in. They were on tiny pieces of cardboard, about the size of a postcard. They were the highlight of my day if I was at home, which I invariably was, seated at the low table eating soft-boiled eggs, drinking cans of warmed coffee and typing away.

I often tried to analyse the reasons for why I enjoyed receiving bills in this country opposed to my homeland, where such correspondence would commonly strike me down with stress, anxiety and general displeasure. What it came down to is a complete lack of awareness as to the content of the 'slips.' I didn't understand any of it. Sure, I had learned some rudimentary Japanese while stationed here in self-imposed exile, I even had a decent grasp of Hiragana characters, but those 'slips' in their oppressive formal Kanji, forget about it. The joy in receiving them did not stem from trying to decipher the garbled messages of my various utility accounts, the pleasure and relief as those pictographs washed over me lay in the very fact that I did not have to understand the message at all. All I needed to comprehend was the amount and the due date. Any and all agency stripped from my Self. It was the pure, unquestionable action of accepting these bills for what they were that set free my soul. I had no need to argue with anyone about being overcharged for something, no pointless hours of waiting on call centre lines around the world to debate 'on peak' vs. 'off peak' charges, no reference of comparison with rival services to devote my time to. None of these things were options for me anymore. They had been terminated. Eliminated with care and kindness from some power residing above.

Sartre maintained that responsibility was one of the cornerstones of the Anglo-man in his quest to exist. I was never good at responsibility. Not that I didn't have the capacity to be responsible, just that I preferred not to be, that I didn't value it as important. But what I really feared was the responsibility of choosing. I feared reading and comprehending information that required action. I feared finding out things were not as cost-effective or ethically acceptable to a consumer as they perhaps should be. Knowing that I would have to do something about this now that my brain had processed the information. Not wanting to, but being forced to by society, by what people told me to believe in back home, what they taught me – that such trivial things are important. That they are worthy of caring about when they are not. That I should get my money's worth. But what if I preferred to avoid the fight, to just accept things as they were, to not quarrel over money and just forfeit it to a multinational company? Why not let them have it and concentrate on other things? Why not just continue to live, without confrontation? This mentality, mine that is, was not acceptable growing up in the white, middle-class suburb of a Western democracy. In Japan, everything changed though. I was not expected to understand, I was not expected to fight. An expansive translucent cultural and linguistic barrier was erected. It prevented me from being able to know these things, from processing this useless information. It protected and insulated my brain from the knowledge of responsibility, of agency, of choice. So, when those 'slips' rolled in every second Thursday, I didn't have to choose. I didn't have to talk to anyone. I didn't have to pretend to care while I argued with some migrant worker in a third-world country earning less than minimum wage. Neither of us had to keep up the charade. All of it was taken away from me. I merely had to take the 'slip' down to a convenience store, wait patiently in line and pay the amount it told me to. Until the next Thursday when the white-gloved mailman would show up to my premises to kickstart the process all over again. With the beautiful clunk of cardboard on metal.

PINK LIGHT TRANCE OUT

*****

My new neighbour always got home late. So late that the only sounds he had to contend with were the tinkling pipes and the calming hum of electrical appliances on standby. The walls were tripwire thin and every night at some unholy hour you would hear him switch on the television as he let the abrasive tones of local variety shows loose into the surrounding air. His default mode challenged my ears on the nightly. I had never seen him before, but I pictured a bedraggled nondescript Asian man with an anguished facial expression slumping onto his futon, letting the canned laughter wash over him while he presumably consumed his cup noodles in a drunken torpor, the odd inflection of the host's speech lulling him into a meditative trance out. Helping him forget his life full of painful blows in a luminous glow. His habits reminded me of the raucous, but familiar, scratching of a possum that has decided to nest in the cavities of a roof. Although never visually observed, the repetitive nature of the sounds were enough to strike up an unlikely kinship. I even thought of giving him a name.

There were few exceptions to the deafening holocaust of variety show audio I had to endure when it came to the nocturnal sounds emitted from my neighbouring partition. A quite notable one occurred once a month. This decadent set of audio samples belonged to a phenomenon that the Japanese quite aptly titled 'delivered health.' It involved companionship of the female variety. It was the kind of import necessary for men that flirted on the edge of the hikikomori cloud. The kind of mandatory mental support required when modern society is in the process of working you to death – an array of ever-mounting menial tasks usurping any ability to socially relate or connect with other living things.

A diet of sex, death and variety shows.

The first time it occurred, my most immediate thought was that it was an incredibly strange feeling not to awake to the familiar variety show cacophony. This had become part of my routine, like brushing my teeth or folding up a sleeve that was too long. It was deeply ingrained. My neighbour's habits had slowly become a part of me. Laying still amongst the silent querelles of the night, instead I heard what sounded like a high school girl weeping. A continuous descending pitiful whining. Not dissimilar to that of a pouting girl that hasn't got her way. It took some time for me to accurately place the rhythm of these utterances into any coherent explanation for what was happening next door. Casting my mind to anime 'pornography' that I had 'sociologically' consumed before, I came to realise this light simpering was supposed to indicate a pleasurable experience. At that point, I knew exactly what was going on.

I was still in shock when I recalled the event the following day. Could it be that this lonely specimen had a lover? A woman that was fond of a man who couldn't say no to a cheap drink and the bitter taste of common post-midnight variety shows? I expressed my concerns aloud to Damien the next day, describing my neighbour's regular routine and last night's exception to the rule.

"Ah. Delivered health." He muttered following a perfunctory grunt.

"What? You mean, like, prostitution?"

"Yes. The company will dispatch a girl at your request to your home or hotel or other designated place to provide sexual massage. Sexual relief, some call it."

'Sexual' massage. Is that what all the whimpering was about? Had my neighbour indulged in a 'sexual' massage? Relief, if you will.

"Blowjobs, handjobs, footjobs... Whatever the client wants." Damien went on amiably.

"Your friend must really be sick." He sucked his teeth. "Don't worry, it's normal. We all are."

I contemplated my neighbour's position. Neglected, still needing human touch despite the fact he had seemingly transcended the requirement in a solitary storm of cup noodles and late-night advertisements. My savvy neighbour, 'dialling in,' ordering some health to go. No unnecessary thinking or moving required. Simple, effective momentary pain relief from society's usual tonic. You had to hand it to him. He was a master.

Over the following weeks, the muted tones of interviews with J-Pop stars wafted through the open balcony window confirming that my neighbour had reverted to the usual unfettered stream of 3am variety shows. After Damien's description of 'delivered health' though, and the memory of that high-pitched snivelling emanating from the grooves of the partition, I could hardly get the concept out of my mind.

It was then I began researching in earnest the various Methods of

Shimei. All the different customs in which a wayward person could obtain 'delivered health.' I began to sympathise with my neighbour's desires. I was doing fine on my own, but I never knew when I wouldn't be doing so fine. Sometimes, you just need a beautiful human body breathing next to you. Living, looking, listening. All of those things. You never knew when you might need all those 'special' things delivered in a package to your door.

I found several companies that offered 'English-speaking' services, a large number of them employing this tag ceremonially based on the poorly transcribed website content. I reviewed all of them online. I read through unreal descriptions of what was on offer. I used Google Translate where necessary. I scaled and traversed the peaks and troughs of various perverted message boards. I had the power to freely choose a girl I wanted to spend 'special' time with. Delivery of health directly to my apartment was coalescing into a very real option.

Several Saturdays and moons later, I was shocked again to be awoken by all the sounds I ordinarily never hear. The simpering and miserable off-kilter giggling was back. I calmly collected my thoughts and extracted my laptop from my bag. The homepage of the chosen service had already been bookmarked during my research. The review site 'Osaka Bros' said they only took half an hour. I automatically filled in my details and provided my credit card number. I pressed enter. I clicked next. I received a message in a separate tiny window that popped up. There was a bunch of Japanese text beneath the word 'success.' My fate was pre-determined.

I settled in to listen to the heartbroken murmurs from next door. Blowjob? Handjob? Footjob? Mouthjob? Job-job? Which one was it to be?

When she arrived, she did not exude confidence. She was pretty and slightly corpulent. Her expressions were shy, anxiety rising in her face like a confused field mouse that finds itself at the entrance of a recreational swimming pool. The smell of bodies and chlorine striking a profound feeling of uncertainty into its small soul.

I asked her to sit. We made attempts at conversing with no real progress. The weather, the night, the Japan – how were they all? They were all fine. They were all good. ~5 minutes passed before I told her what I wanted to do.

"Do you know ba-rai-tee-sho?"

"Ng," she managed to mumble, nodding incessantly.

It was 3:34am. The broken puppy sounds had ceased from the adjacent apartment. My neighbour had seemingly finalised his transaction. I, however, had not.

I picked up the seldom used remote and turned on the cost-effective, medium-sized television that came with the rented apartment. I only ever used it to watch pro-wrestling and critically analyse the organised insanity of Japanese commercials while I ate pre-packaged meals from the convenience store located on the apartment complex's ground floor. I channel-surfed and cranked the volume. I was on the search for canned laughter, I craved the irritating tones of a nasally variety show host. I yearned to finally feel it. What it was that he felt.

Sitting. Watching. Observing. I had no idea what they were saying, though the girl seemed to relax substantially. Yes, she was having a good time. A shredded ray of sunshine in what she assumed would be another dismal day. I continued to turn the volume up until it was 75% 'cranked'. I procured a bag of dried squid to munch on and watched the shit out of this show I would never see again. I watched it tense and hard for ~25 minutes. I focused intently on the facial expressions of the host. I photographically observed the miniscule lines and creases stemming from the mouths of Japanese stars that were interviewed in the 'hot' seat. I became the sound of the elongated vowels and honorific suffixes of the talking heads on the screen. I no longer felt human. I was pure being.

When I disengaged from my daze, she was exiting my apartment quietly, careful not to disrupt the flow of the night. She fumbled over her gratitude and courtesy as Japanese girls are prone to do. Then she was gone. I turned down the volume of the television, which had now moved on to some sort of cooking program, and roughly unplugged the set. I moved to the confines of my bed. I lay under the covers inertly as I strained to hear the movements of my fellow spirit behind the wall. No variety shows. No 'delivered health.' Just the unmistakable ever-so-slight murmuring of a grown man as he cries.

I stayed with a random girl I was seeing the following week. She didn't own a television set and neither did I. I contemplated buying one from a pawn shop for her, but it ultimately proved too much work. I haven't used the 'delivered health' service since, but I kept the page bookmarked. I assure myself that one day the timing will be right to re-enact the teachings of my neighbour as I seek to counteract the submerged lights of my inner loneliness.

DISRUPTION OF FLOW

*****

Without a job, or a relationship or any responsibility, I find myself on the internet a lot at night. Sometimes, during these dark computer sessions, I feel there is a blank mass obstructing my flow. It looms over me like a magnified cursor that hovers above one of the ubiquitous social media pleasure-feeds. Like a thirsty seed of mustard. Like a damp katsu sando purchased from the convenience store at 3:34am.

To dislodge this ever-present lack of clarity, I need to rid myself of all that my online history knows. The disgusting truth of the wasted 'intelligence' I have gathered. Forget the bookmarked memories, the external hard drives overflowing with files in .mp3 .mkv .avi .png .jpg .doc .pdf that I have downloaded, accumulated and saved over the years that I will never open again.

Bury the myriad online personas I curate.

Burst from the digital chrysalis at year zero.

Re-ignite my Self from the archaic start.

Yet I know this will not occur. The object that obfuscates my thoughts must stay. Leaving it behind is too strenuous, too overwhelming – ultimately, it is too much work. It will remain there, wedged in my throat, imprinted on my brain, melded to my heart as I stumble blindly into online trends, replicated memes, artificial personalities, toxic likes, mindless threads. These things are me, whether I like it or not.

The disruption of flow is not a detour I have to work around – it is an addiction I subconsciously crave, a hunger I fundamentally need. To remove this from my life would be psychologically shattering, arguably catastrophic – the hollowness of my true being open for all to see.

It is always easier not to think. Browsing swiping scrolling automatic on autopilot avionic totally submissive. A necessary aversion to confrontation. A better alternative than trying to feel. To avert the inevitable, the difficult – the mass obstructing my flow must stay. Forever clogging my mental path.

SPACE FOR THE DISEMBODIED AND DISCARNATE

* * * * *

Today, I need to find work. I am taking the train. I like the train system here, its raison d'être. It fits my worldview – that conversations uttered aloud should not be permitted on trains. People should have the right to sit and listen to the ambience of the electric motor humming, the repetitive clack of the tracks under wheel while they are enveloped by the passing milieux of scenes as they go by.

In Japan, this is understood. The train ride is a sacred ritual for the disembodied and discarnate. When you enter this space, a metaphorical sign hanging from your neck materialises. It says: 'Please, don't interrupt me.' An unspoken rule shared between passengers for differing periods of time. Not to be broken under any circumstances. Everyone aware that this transitional space allows the necessary room to gain what little strength can be mustered as they temporarily reconstruct themselves. Cognizant that it is critical to replenish dwindling health levels before re-emerging to face the oppressive world outside the carriage's confines.

The natural process of breaking and making links with the shared 'accidental others' obliterated when the frivolous social chattering of the dismal world above enters this muted channel.

PASSENGERS

* * * * *

I alight at the exchange. Exchange after exchange. Shotgun images of foot soldiers holding sweat-ridden hand towels. Disseminated visions of cheap polyester suits. Shuddering carriages impregnate my mind. Any cogent thought annihilated by the rabid hiss of hydraulic brakes. My transmigration to destination one complete. Slip into the elevator before it closes. Revel amid a sea of pockmarked skin and dead fish lips. Occupants decked out in downtrodden trousers from the local emporium. Prizes claimed from the city's myriad pockets of null zone pits.

Yellow fingers under lengthy nails. No one available to give them a clip. Literal torrents of cigarette mountains. Shovelling curry rice with bare hands result in permanent stains. Legions of translucent umbrellas imperceptibly undulate as the elevator ascends. History of what the tea leaves show exposed. Opalescent discs of fellow passengers flicker wide. My appearance belies I'm one of the tribe. Breathe in the fumes of the enclosed cabin. Cheap alcohol emitted from Asian skin. Suck in the particles of reeking air. I can smell all sixty years.

Extract the coins from my pockets. Creased flesh of exposed eponychium encrusted in grime. Shower the ticket machines with my lust. Defer command to the transportation overlords. We all need to get from A to B. Sometimes even to C. Let's not even fucking talk about D. Exclaim to the others that I can see what they see. I am not an apparition. I am not at all so different. From near or far, we are all forced to show our respect for the system. Play the game or be ordained to the confines of a cardboard box. Submit or die.

Knowing half-smiles under floppy 100 Yen hats. Key chains of worn-out anime characters under artificial light. Cockroaches lapping up sake in dark concrete corners. Fibrous sclera become our shared open admission. Faint insinuations of laughter permeate the troposphere. Not the Japan you know, they say silently. I know, I know, my eyes echo. When they get to the Go parlour or Pachinko monoliths to meet with their buddies, their voices buried in a lurid cacophony, I hope they say it. I hope they tell the truth. That they looked into the eyes of a lost gaijin at the station today and he knew. That the history of this country is just the same as everywhere else. No different. Not special. Full of people trying to hold the snow globe of existence together in the face of a listless tsunami. So sick and tired that no one is shaking it.

Let's suck our collective discoloured teeth in unison.
Let's talk about the weather because there isn't anything else to say.
Let's exclaim loudly how good food tastes while obnoxiously shoving it down our expectant throats.
Let's stare into the commercialised void of our television sets and collectively give in.
Let's pay a visit to the convenience store and buy the cheapest bottle of liquor we can afford.
Because what else do we have to believe in?

EMPLOYMENT I

* * * * *

After like six weeks, I got a job as an English teacher. It was a relatively new school. Word at the bars I frequented was it had grown rapidly in popularity due to its radical model and ruthless promotion. The company was called Dainichi, named after the supreme cosmic Buddha from a strand of 'esoteric' Buddhism, which was a peculiar name for an English school. This was par for the course in Japan, where there was some sort of unwritten rule that you couldn't promote an English school without christening it with an awfully weird name. I'm not sure what compelled the imposing creators of these schools to come up with these names, but I guess they had their reasons. My theory was the more obscure the name, the bigger the creator's ego. Not that I had anything concrete to back that up, but I liked to think I was right. I researched the name Dainichi online after I got the job and found that the word also meant 'great sun' and that the supreme cosmic Buddha integrated the six elements of earth, water, fire, wind, space and consciousness with the activities of body, speech and mind. After finding out the meaning behind the word, I was certain that the creators of the school possessed massive ego's in line with my obscure name theory. This theory would prove true over time as I was gradually introduced to the inaugural team of managers who exhibited various degrees of narcissistic personality disorders.

Getting a job at Dainichi meant I had to buy clothes as I didn't really have anything suitable for such an occasion. Which was strange, because I planned to live here indefinitely, and we all know that means you gotta pull your finger out of the stinking chum bucket and earn some cold-hard bones. Clams. Wing-wangs. Whatever colloquial term the cool kids called it these days. I couldn't even recall what I wore at the job interview. It was one of those cultish lab-mouse activity-based ones. The ones designed by marketers masquerading as neuroscientists to weed out people that lack 'innovation.' The selection criteria somewhat ambiguously based on how good-looking you are and how many buzzwords you can use in the group session. If you are relatively well-educated, and not hideously ugly, it's easy enough to luck your way through it. However, there were a few stiffs in the session that didn't get the memo. Tall, thin beanpoles with smudge-marked glasses that treated the whole thing far too seriously. Dainichi didn't want serious though. They wanted genki, witty, charming people. The interviewers didn't give a shit whether you knew a vowel from a consonant as long as some rich Japanese person wanted to ogle you while talking about their designer hobbies.

My quest for adequate clothing inevitably led me to Don Quijote, or 'Donki' as it was known, basically a huge mega-mart with all sorts of ordinary, and not so ordinary, paraphernalia on sale. I was certain they would have cost-effective work pants for a miserable price. Ill-fitting for sure, but probably sufficiently passable for my newfound role as a semi-respectable member of Japanese society. They might even have English labelling on the tag for easy identification of garment size. Sure enough, once I passed the signposted markers for Tenga eggs, sex pillows, fake facial hair and customised Subaru gear-knobs resembling Slurpee-filled dildos I arrived at the more conservative men's clothing section of the store. It was easy enough to find black slack-like pants, however, the tags and size guide were not in English. Not even Romaji, the Romanised version of the Japanese language. This is what I was secretly afraid of. Despite being what I would consider a relatively 'smart' guy, the foreign language part of my brain was constantly blanketed by a thick fog. I had tried out a few different methods of learning elementary Japanese, but ultimately my mind sucked at processing and recalling even basic information. The grammar and vocabulary forever plunged in thick molasses. Furthermore, I couldn't take the slightest hit when I tried to articulate something out loud. My voice microscopic and pathetic. The syllables barely audible as I struggled to express simple requests like "where is the toilet?" or "no bags please." All self-esteem and confidence completely obliterated by my hyper-anxiety. I was too scared to find a staff member at the store, overtly concerned that I couldn't coherently express what I needed to say with body language alone. I hastily procured a pair of pants from the rack and held them aloft to my rigid legs, hoping to some benevolent power they would fit. I bought the pants in a whirlwind not dissimilar to a manic episode experienced by someone with bipolar as they spiral into an impulsive spending spree – instantly regretting this pang of self-medication when they snap out of their reverie days later. When I arrived home, one try of the pants clearly showed they didn't fit. It seemed that my fears were realised. I would have to return to the store.

On the second attempt at pants shopping I arrived at Donki well-prepared. My flip phone didn't have browser access and my smart phone didn't work outside the wi-fi zone of my apartment, so I was essentially Google-less. However, I had all the Katakana and Hiragana written out on a tiny pastel blue piece of paper for key sizing words like 'waist' and 'length' and 'width.' I had studied the pants at great length and was self-assured I knew which size to grab with my keen hands given my knowledge of how the previous pair fit. I wanted to avoid confrontation and embarrassment as much as possible, so I opted to cop the 2000 Yen on the nose and keep the pants that didn't fit. I couldn't bring myself to deal with the returns section of the store knowing it would mean mouse-like squeaks of Japanese whilst the staff member and I stood around looking broken and confused.

Upon reaching the men's work attire section, I started to panic. The brand of pants I purchased last time were nowhere to be seen. A new rack of men's black pants had replaced the previous style and model. The labels were all different. The numbers, the katakana, the hiragana… It was all fucking different. I had been taken for a ride. I was truly and utterly defeated once again. In a haze, I returned to the previous method used with the last pair of pants. Rigid legs… Held aloft… Eyeball the length… Palms beaded with sweat… As I paid for this second pair of work pants, my body language and demeanour were already resigned to my fate – I was destined for another pair of ill-fitting trousers. The staff member may have asked me if I was sure, but I didn't hear, I had reached the brink of no return. I dropped the money on the clerk's plastic tray at the register and barely remembered to pick up my change. I didn't even try the pants on when I got home. I threw them straight into the plastic set of 100 Yen drawers in the wardrobe, bag and all, knowing that I had to face my reservations and formulate a new pants plan.

I decided that I would try a different store on attempt three. I had already forfeited almost 5000 Yen worth of shame trying to purchase a pair of pants, what else did I have to lose? I decided to give in and shell out a bit more money. My body dragging me to a place where I would not feel uncomfortable using English. I chose a Uniqlo store on a dense shopping street in a touristy area. The sizes were clear and easy to distinguish. The labels all had English. I could use the changerooms without having to talk to anyone. I just followed the sign in the store. It outlined the location of the changerooms in five different languages. A staff member gave me a coloured slot that indicated how many items I had chosen to try on. I didn't need to utter a word. I couldn't bear to look at the staff member. Couldn't bring myself to exchange smiles.

The first pair of pants fit like a perfectly rolled cigar. I wouldn't have the money to be back here for a while, so it was crucial I made the most of this unique opportunity. My confidence was sky high. I was on a major roll. Peaking from the snugness of the pants, I even built up the courage to grab a few shirts. When I left the store, the high of my success quickly dissipated. Memories of the previous misfires still plagued me, the bastard trousers folded and untouched in my drawers.

*****

Though the job itself was quite unremarkable, the setting and format were almost indescribable. The English 'school' was set in a high-rise office and each 'instructor' had their own cubicle, exactly like an office. The lighting was constantly set low, the music tuned to classical jazz. There was even a reception area for students to comfortably wait for their lesson to begin. Attractive staff members clad in black served them steaming green tea or espresso while they browsed glossy magazines punctuated with intermittent characters of English and Japanese. There was a huge iridescent Coca-Cola billboard outside the window on the westside of the building. It was just like the one in Blade Runner. I often requested to be situated on this side of the building where I could stare interminably at the Coca-Cola sign, wishing endlessly that the red and white pixels would propel me into the throes of a fictional future. A future where I didn't have to face the regret of being myself. Gazing at the sign, it made me feel how absurd it was to teach another language in such a setting. The pulsating cursive of the familiar logo piercing the façade of my questionable motifs.

The lessons worked like this. You would log on to an online portal and identify which blocks of 45 minutes you were available for students to book your lessons. Each 'instructor' had a profile with a photograph, some basic information about them like which country they were from and a little quirky blurb at the bottom to give the student an idea of what kind of lesson/personality they were in for. You were meant to really sell yourself. Your experience, your brand, your spitting uniqueness. Students would either book lessons online or call the company to select an instructor based on their availability and personal preference. When the students arrived for their lesson, they were given a booth number that corresponded with the pod their instructor was assigned for the day. The students would wait in the reception area until an innocuous bell chimed indicating it was time for their lesson to begin. This chime would signal the instructor to be upstanding, as if they were royally saluting a flag or posing for an important school photograph, trying their best to look enthusiastic as their student's face materialised in the corridor amongst a sea of shifting bodies. The lesson would cover an introduction, a unit from an online 'textbook' based on the student's level of comprehension, and culminated in feedback for the student at the end. Instructors were encouraged to write little handwritten notes for the students to take away with them as mementos of their precious time. In true Japanese style, the lessons would never run short nor long. You were guaranteed that the charade would go on for the full 45 minutes. At the conclusion of the lesson, the omnipresent chime would ring out again. This was the cue for the instructor and student to part ways. There was a five-minute interval for instructors to finalise their notes from the previous lesson and then that soothing chime would hit again, like a velvet sledgehammer, indicating it was time for the next student's round, upstanding with dignity, ready to do it all over again.

*****

There were a lot of strange individuals at the workplace. All of them had it together enough to act professionally in front of the managers and students, however, when you discussed things with them in between classes it was clear there was something a little off. Some unknown insect that had burrowed beneath the skin of their face and settled in. Something manifestly ill trepanning their brain. We all shared it – the persistence of a hungry six-legged living thing residing somewhere in our deep, dank corners. You had to be a little off to leave the well-set dream of conformity behind.

There was this one guy named Clement. He was from Hong Kong and wanted desperately to be Japanese. He craved it. Changed his citizenship, passport, the works. Word was that he completely submitted to his Japanese wife and family who were extremely traditional. You got the sense from talking to him that he had completely sold out his own culture. He was smug and dishonest. An utter piece of shit. He followed the blue suit-brown belt-brown shoe combination that so many obdurate Japanese young men subscribed to. He was uptight and under the thumb. He had the kind of smile you wanted to wipe off with a coarse piece of sandpaper. Given any opportunity, he would knife you and wrench it hard. Bowing and nodding politely to the company's superiors while he twisted the blade to extract maximum juice out of his latest victim.

There was this hot Russian girl who was young and told stories about all the people she fucked. I never learned her name. She seemed to fornicate with a different person every night. She would arrive to the office bleary-eyed in the mornings ready to spill her guts about her latest conquests. The male students loved her. She would brag about all the ones she bedded just before you were due to teach them, leaving you with a remark about the size of their phallic member or their favourite fetish just before the bell chimed and the student rushed in. She would whisper shit like: "Hiroki-san has a 45-degree kink in his cock" before rushing off to her pod. At times like those, there wasn't anything else you could do but use your imagination.

A fan-favourite amongst students was this middle-aged Mexican dude named Ricardo. He kind of looked like a member of the Mexican aristocracy. He wore sparkling gold vests and had a collection of coloured pens for his private lessons. His schedule was jam-packed with people who wanted to ask him questions about Mexico and admire his shiny tuxedos. The little piece of lesson paper they received covered in rainbow drawings of the hour's lesson. His English was awful though. I once overheard him tell a student that 'maybe' was a stronger certainty of prediction than 'definitely.' But it didn't matter. Like I said before, no one was interested in the technicalities of right or wrong, they were here for the validation, the dollars, the need to be anywhere else but alone in their homes.

Then there was Cooper, he was from America and he would leave cans of chuhai in the shared refrigerator to see what management would say. He was one impeccably smooth sailor. We would go outside to smoke joints and shotgun beers when we both had a 'free' lesson. A 'free' lesson meant no one booked us. I secretly hoped hardly anyone booked me for the lessons I made myself available. Then I could either walk around doing shit by myself or go and do something stupid with Cooper. Sometimes, I would just go and photocopy art books at the convenience store. The only problem with these 'free' lessons was that they were exactly that – free. In other words, you didn't get paid for them. The best type of lesson was when someone booked you and then didn't show up. This way you would still get paid for the lesson and you wouldn't even have to pretend to do any work. This would happen more often than you'd think, as the clientele were all affluent and could afford to throw money away. Sometimes parents would sign up their twenty-something year old kid to a twelve-lesson package and the kid would basically just ditch every time. The same thing would happen with businesses that paid for their employees to learn English in this forum. Often the salarymen foot soldiers wouldn't even have time to attend their prepaid lessons due to sixteen hour shifts at the metropolitan office hellhole.

Most of the employees were pure seekers of justification. All they wanted was to be fed compliments. They lived for the artificial smiles. Clement, the Russian girl, Ricardo – they didn't care if it was all a fake parade. They pretended it was real. Pretended that there was genuine love for them.

You needed a gimmick to be successful though. I struggled to book lessons out primarily for this reason – I was middle-class, white, male, boring. I had no gimmick. There was nothing unique about me in the eyes of the students – I wasn't from Africa, I didn't know any magic tricks and I certainly couldn't be fucked using coloured pens. I was like a pro-wrestler with no charisma. Destined to ply my trade putting people over in the mid-card.

Most of the vapid students who came to my lessons either didn't specify which instructor they wanted or selected me just to 'try me out.' This was a common tactic of the regulars. Some of the students were insane, but they had money, so the company accepted their business. Without capital, their behaviour would have resulted in them being ejected from the building. There was one extremely interesting dude who loved to talk about how many war criminals were still alive in Japan. He couldn't help but stir the delicious pot. Most people hated him, because he made the lesson uncomfortable with his politically incorrect rants, but I thought he was awesome.

He basically paid you to ramble on about how messed up Imperial Japan was for 45 minutes until the bell chimed for the end of his lesson.

Most other students were seemingly quite dull, following the entrenched hierarchical rules of their culture – taking out lifetime loans for apartments in sought after locations, watching television shows about the best ramen joints etc. I learned a lot about the human condition and our shared neurosis from both the teachers and students at Dainichi. That we were all just trying things out, testing the water of existence in hope that we could find something tolerable to commit to, but also something acceptable to the people and society that defined our existence. The whole thing - work, social interaction, career – it was all just one big try. Dainichi solidified this for me. Maybe the origins of the company's name were not as obscure as I initially thought. The supreme cosmic Buddha, the great sun – perhaps it had taught me something. The ability to integrate the six elements of being into the activities of my body, speech and mind.

YOUR 7:45PM CLASS HAS BEEN CANCELLED

*****

Elevator down from ten.
Get off at six.
Turn right at the end of the corridor.

Squeeze your eyes tight and try to remember. Vision behind the lids missing key components – filled in with what the mind can only logically assume would be there in the myriad gaps of consciousness. Small, distinct dots of differing colours coalesce into a pattern that forms a whole. Worthy of whatever was the original.

Open your eyes.
Blink.
Keep walking on autopilot.

*****

Past a large window overlooking the street below, a scent of perfume and running water, like that found in the lobby of a high-class hotel, wafts over me. Dim lights running parallel to a mauve strip of patterned carpet show me the way to my playground.

Escalator descends. The aroma remains. Inoffensive jazz plays softly from the speakers overhead. Nothing about the music remotely experimental. Nothing to jar the senses. Urging the 'right' people to stay. The people that can merely function as if they are the 'right' people – the purposeful clientele the labyrinth of consumption desires. A minotaur looms, manifesting in the form of a phantom, not visible but present in each of their souls as they loiter in the neutral space between identical retail zones. Somewhere here, the demarcation lies. Walking amongst them, the temporary owners of these segments of non-locales reside chittering with faux pleasure.

Past an upmarket hi-fi store, bored inveterate employees suck on lemonade flavoured candy. They patiently await the next drive-by to wind down the window of their frontal cortex and let them take a peek at their preferences. These well-dressed clerks consistently seek to deftly breach the targets' lower pleasure regions. But this is not a used car lot, brute force and underhanded tactics are not necessary here. This is where the mindless affluent members of the twenty-first century graze. All nibbles taken more subtly.

Simply looking is enough to integrate the casual window shopper into the sphere of influence unfurled by the ghost in the machine at play here. The crags of husks successfully incorporated into this space to avoid an unceremonious return to their ephemeral cubic living spaces at all costs. It's better for both this way.

An open public space lit by the same soothing LED's that illuminate the path above appear, low mahogany coffee tables and Queen Anne Wingback chairs set in specific positions painstakingly arranged by a mysterious curator. An ensemble of men and women of class scattered about, reading magazines, notarising diary entries, browsing smartphones. Consuming time until the next task is 'assigned.' Then a reminder tone will chime, signalling calmly that it is time to move on to the next pre-determined responsibility.

I know how it feels.
I am one of these people.
It doesn't feel bad, if you know how to play it.

SPERM BUILDING MEET

* * * * *

There was this building on the border of what I defined as the city's 'tourist limits,' kind of where the normal suburban lives began and the glamour of a traveller's short sojourn ended. The building was gold and looked like a giant sperm. Like something from a high school sex education VHS put out by a not-for-profit company. The animated image of the sperm unctuous and dripping as it entered a fictional depiction of the female's egg. I would ride past it on my bicycle or see photographs of it in magazines and think "Yeah, take me to your eggs." Someone once told me it was designed by Philippe Starck, the famous French designer. They went on to say that he should "stick to furniture", which again, made me think about eggs and how they stick to pans.

I met a Japanese girl through work, then added her on Line, then endured her Google translated replies, then somehow agreed to meet her face-to-face at the sperm building. There was a restaurant at the sperm structure, but we didn't eat there. It was far too expensive. Even with a job. We wandered very purposefully, I think, to a Starbucks. Somewhere with familiarity, a place that we thought was equal footing for us both – a respected institution in both our cultures. We split a pack of four sandwich corners with various ingredients inside. We had coffee. She ordered it. I assiduously paid. We couldn't converse very well. It was like the other times. A mixture of submissive nodding and muddled eyes amongst the familiar sounds of 'nggg' and 'eeehhhh' of my never-ending dates.

I remember her saying that because I could say a lot of Japanese food words that she thought I was more Japanese than other Western men she had met. She said something like "I think you want to be Japanese" – but she didn't mean it that way, it was just an inaccurate translation for what she wanted to articulate. I did not harbour any grudges for this. It was my life now. Listening to the imperfect words of people I barely knew.

We walked back to the train station through a large concrete park at dusk. There were glistening water features everywhere, entirely sopping in the surrounding light of halogens and LED's. She was hesitant when it came time to kiss me. She eventually committed to my mouth with her arms dangling by her sides. Those dangling arms made me feel ridiculous. Like, it made me hate why I had to do this. I couldn't believe what was happening to me. What right did I have to meet this girl, put her through a torturous series of deciphered messages and urge her to meet me at the giant golden sperm as we struggled through a skeletal conversation? The bones of our minimal words picked bare by my sexual intentions. I should have called it off. I should have said goodbye in the reflecting lights, her arms remaining comfortably by her sides, but I didn't. I had to make them dangle. All out of the compulsion of my misplaced desire.

She awkwardly left so I started walking toward the train station entrance in the middle of the pitiful evening. I found that it was uncharacteristically dark in the urban Japanese night. I made my way up into the back of the train and as I sat there it was obvious how much it meant to me to be here in Japan on my own, existing on the edge of a city that might have meant something to me, knowing that I was alone.

When I got home, I sent a short message to the girl about how we couldn't see each other anymore. I elaborated on the reasons why – language, culture, distance. I fell asleep in a storm of shame and searched for reasons why I did these things. When I awoke, she had provided a sweetly toned, long-winded, Google translate assisted message saying that she understood. That she was naive to think she could relate to me given our different languages and cultural backgrounds. All of this in disjointed, hard to follow, computer-generated English. I vowed not to do this again, not to put anyone else through this. After lunch though, I found I was already scrolling mindlessly through the holy triumvirate apps in search of the next one. Where I would continue to feel a little joy and a lot of shame.

STRIP CLUB TRAIN STATION

*****

We are all actors. This is what we know. We aspire to be other versions of ourselves. Looking down at ourselves and hoping, wishing we were someone else. Anyone else. Anything else but what we are. We want life to be like a sequence of Instagram images. We crave a carefully constructed reality that doesn't exist and never will. I am at the strip club train station tonight. I feel like I am Bill Murray's character in Lost in Translation, waiting for my Charlotte/Scarlett to show up so we can go to karaoke. I don't really want to be here, I would rather someone whisk me away. But I know that won't be happening. I will remain here, alone, staring into the void of beautiful pussies until I decide to leave and become conjoined with the streets of ice again.

The strip club train station is not called that. I don't know the name of it, but this is what I termed it. I found out about it when a wealthy buddy from Chicago met up with me while he was on a weekly sojourn to Japan. Being a stock broker, he and his sick mineral water imbibing Patrick Bateman crew knew all the gaudy tricks. You entered a slim building in the red-light district and, as you do in Japan, dive into a tiny elevator to ascend to a space that is astoundingly different to what one envisions from the façade. There is a small reception area, nothing spectacular, at first. Past the diaphanous curtains though, once you slip through the wet membrane of this bounded area, lies an exact replica of a metro train carriage. When I say exact, I don't mince the mayo. The seats, the handrails, the hanging straps – it was all there. Full formation. Solid, not gelatinous. My lurid compatriot from Chicago even went so far as to say it was a real carriage that had been decommissioned, deconstructed and somehow re-compiled in this seventh-floor high-rise building in the red-light district. To add to the simulacrum, there is a soundtrack that accompanies the carriage. The soundtrack has been compiled from recordings taken from trains moving between stations. Joints squeaking and jostling, brakes retching and shuttering, hydraulics hissing and suffering. For a large price, that's if you're super-pasta-creepy, you can pay to grope the replica of a real-life Japanese school girl in a real-life setting. Art mimicking life. A safe space for the cosmopolitan city's chikan purveyors. A space to act out their fantasies without losing face, without guilt forcing them to jump in front of the next speeding carriage that looks exactly the same as the one the act is committed in.

That was all a little too morbid for me, perhaps interesting as a sociological experiment for my affluent American friend, but not for everyone. After all, I didn't want to act out some absurd fetish fantasy, I was only here because I felt a little lonely. Same as usual, same as always. Luckily for me, there was a more cost-effective and less disturbing room behind the facsimile carriage. This space wasn't even really a room, it was a kind of miniature butterfly house and garden. It was basically a normal strip club, except women danced on podiums obscured by living ferns and vines. It was a pornographic green house for the down and out and disheartened. Butterflies would flit about, casually landing on the exposed flesh of the employees, images of mesmerising vibrant wings contrasted against the soft honeyed skin of the nubile hosts. To add to the already bizarre setting, the space was tiny. Only two girls and two clients could fit inside at any one time. It was like being in one of those miniscule aquariums for Siamese fighting fish, the ones they sell at the pet shop that invoke sadness, the beautiful creature dancing hypnotically in a diminutive mass of water. The whole thing was immaculate. It was a microscopic Eden on steroids. As time went on, I developed a dreary addiction to the contaminated plants and emotional trip wires of this exotic memory garden.

Tonight, I wait in line with the rest of the fallen warriors, slurping up the aroma of cheap suits reeking of rice-based liquor. There is always a line, but I'm happy to wait. I need a fix from the confines of the locket terrarium. I want to breathe in the rotten air of the perverted masses and hold it tightly, let it marinate in me until I am dizzy and can't go on. This will maximise the ecstasy of the moment when I enter the crystal-encrusted chamber to experience the divine. The stagnant breath of society temporarily vanquished when I fall under the spell of the vivarium queens. Only then will I be released from this version of reality. Version 3.7, the most recent software update. It hasn't made things better. There are still several bugs and glitches that need to be overridden. I need to hold steadfast though as subsequent versions may never come. The development team responsible for system improvements to my soul have come to an oppressive halt.

It is now my turn. I enter the hot-box. The air consumes me. The gossamer leaves caress my turbid form. Shades of emerald, neon-green infect my sight. Trails of pulsating violet beguile my core. I am an insect stuck in the treacle of a tropical pitcher plant. I hear the dim intimation of vaguely tribal music. I get high off the sap that lines the calyx as her nebulous form begins to dance. Taken completely in by the host's waxy scales and cuticular folds, every aqueous move ensures I cannot climb out of her infinite pitcher. And I don't want to. I am content to die here. Asphyxiated by the beauty of her lunate cells. Mesmerised by my very own mandatory glass serpent.

Our figures move in rhythm. My skin is gently provoked by her inward and downward pointing retrorse hairs. Her skin is dewy and warm. I am being drowned in amniotic fluid. My body is gradually being dissolved. Protruding aldehyde crystals shimmer down on my shoulders, my back, like stars being shaken from the sky. I look up through the noxious canopy clouds arrested with her eyes. They tell stories of coral patterns in lunar tides. Our bodies moving, life and landform loops glowing outside of time, I become submerged by the waves of her crescendo. It is time for my private moon to rise.

There is a crystal hymn transmission reverberating in my hollow bones. The urge to terraform my body is avid, real. To submit and become another victim of the passive pitfall of carnal desire. This is what I am doing. Engorging myself on water saturated enzymes secreted from the hairy purple-white striped lid, the tone comes at me in sonar whitecaps. Her movement modifying the hostile atmosphere as the dancing and music swells, grows increasingly faster. I yearn to be ever-transformed. As the jungle dance reaches its conclusion, my inner topography becomes entirely warped. My time is up. I blink and wipe away the sweat. I bat several incandescent butterflies out of my line of sight as I wobble towards the terminus, my deepest cavity filled with hot liquid.

I push my way through the lengthy line-up of odds and sods awaiting the temptations of the Goddess's greenhouse. I pass the gauzy curtain to exit the strip club train station and don't look back. My pants are wet and soiled. I descend floors, numbed and electrically-charged. When the elevator reaches street level, I practically collapse. Head whirling, I tilt it to take in the pantheon of flashing lights. Translucent ghosts bathed in the glow of faux neon signs approach me from both sides. Like them, I must force myself to begin to walk. Aimless, directionless, motionless. Somewhere. There's somewhere I've just gotta go. I stop at the entrance to the nearest metro station. There are no stars or darkness in the sky. It is apparent this reality doesn't exist. We are all actors, but not the Bill Murray kind. The skin of our faces represents a mask. Clinging to whatever surface it can adhere to in order to slip by.

FORTUNE I

* * * * *

Conjoined with the city's streets of ice again. Familiar square lanterns in darkened doorways. Peripatetic aroma of radiant ghosts. The smell of incense is exquisite. My presence will disrupt the flow of energy. The 'gift' of prescience is what I seek.

Time to lure an Omikuji from the box. Fortune-telling paper strips give me a sign of where to look. Pay 100 Yen to shake the paint-by-number box of sticks. Remove one stick. Read the lucky number aloud. Put the stick back in the box. Select my paper from the numbered drawer. Here comes the impression of my fate. Time for the stars to tell me the colour of this underlying aura. How about a middle blessing or a half curse? I'm not here to deal in absolutes. Give me mediocrity. What I already have in spades. It's all I have left. But how is it all that remains? Is there some other element of me that's missing so badly?

Let's not make another big deal out of this, shall we?

Here I am again...

I'm trying not to cry.

I'm not even sure which piece of debris I grab hold of while I choose the stick. The moment you grasp such a magical object at this hour and start pulling yourself up, you can't even remember how you fell to the ground.

When I squint closely at the paper, I can see an Omikuji with a human face. I'm not sure how far a stick can reach into the heavens, but this Omikuji has a human face, this is what I know. And what I have decided is this message will become my destiny. I don't know exactly what occurs when you pick up the stick. I don't know what happens when the stick falls out of the box. I don't know what it does to the world when a stick falls around you. When the paper is extracted from the numbered drawer, I don't even notice I'm holding it in front of me – it's just there. That's my life today.

Chinese zodiac, blood types, Feng Shui... There are even magazines devoted to this shit. How can they be wrong? Birthdays, I Ching, tarots – I'm ill, I'm dying. Give it to me. Give it all to me. Visual perception, palmistry, dream interpretation – someone needs to touch my consciousness. To alter it permanently, please. It's the only way. I'm tired of seeing pictures of me staring stupidly at the world around me (the world as it once was). I want to see my world as it is now. Maybe I'm too exhausted to see the future, or maybe I'm too tired to recall memories of any faces that are important to me. Could I even remember one?

The world I write about is full of images, and I want to have a place to store them. I want to know my life well and see that it's beautiful. That there is beauty and meaning and joy in its contradictions, in pain and suffering and in all of the possibilities that might manifest in my life. It is perhaps why I have come here, to Japan, because I'm tired of the idea that nothing in this world is as it is, that my dreams might not be dreams, or my experience does not mirror that of any other human experience. I am here because I want the soul of Queen Himiko to course through my blood. I desire just a little juice from the baddest bitch on the planet. I demand a little more, something to take the pain away, to give me some peace on both ends of the planet.

Maybe this cheap whiskey I hold is the juice of Queen Himiko.

"I will need a little more." I say and take a swig of the juice.

It makes me feel stupid and empty and it doesn't help that the taste just makes me crave more. Fuck, I can't do this. I take another swig of the juice, then another. I want it to go down faster than the last time. I want it to really fucking hurt.

I drain the flask of Himiko juice. I pocket the Omikuji. I can't bear to read the inscription of my destiny. Not here. Not like this. I pay for the services of a modern-day street shaman instead. ¥5,000. ¥10,000. It doesn't matter to me. It's just like paying for a plate of sashimi in Ginza. Much the same, much the muchness. I want a romance-related reading. I want to feel what it is to be a Japanese woman in her mid-twenties. I want to know whether I will be loved. To look another person in the eye and be informed that I am destined to live out my numbered days alone.

I am shitfaced. I am expectant. I am continuously crying. I tell the street shaman that one time, I had a dream I was lost in Kansai international airport. In the dream, I extract a flight ticket out of my wallet and walk under towering broken glass escalators for hours. Oneiric me feels like he has been stuck in the airport for eternity. The airport is so big and crowded. It feels like I am peering down at the scene from some gigantic tower with an eye-catching rainbow of lights. The image of polychromatic lights eventually recedes back in on itself until an outline of a seat emerges. I realise I am sitting in the seat, on my plane, ready to take off to a destination I do not know. I recall that I lucidly felt so small in the giant seat's emptiness. When I awoke, I had lost all sense of my perspective. It was then I realised I had no body, and nothing inside me but hollowness.

In broken English, the street shaman said the dream gave me a second chance to live my life from a new vantage point. I was asked to meditate. I was asked to become one with the image of the airport in the dream. I meditated. I meditated. Shit, I meditated, I think. I don't know. I was drunk on Himiko's juice. At the end, I thought I had become a real human being – in the same way that the image of the airport reminded me that I was the world I saw in the dream. Barren yet reflective. I looked around me, at the frayed lanterns, at her paunchy face, at the billowing smoke of the incense as the last image of the airport disappeared, replaced by an image of the Japanese city I was living in. I wasn't aware of what the hallucination was about, but when it had passed, I felt the city had a new look to it. And I was one of its people. The street shaman said that I was experiencing something of my own personal history and whatever this was, it was the truth.

I walked outside into the unsophisticated air and gulped in some of the real world's atmosphere. I took the Omikuji from my pocket and breathed a short, stilted sigh. I looked down at the scrunched piece of paper and realised I couldn't read the lines. I ran back down the alley lined with lanterns where the modern-day street shaman was situated. I must have run the wrong direction, or she was gone, or I guess I was too inebriated. Maybe all three. After circling the alleyways, for what my pre-paid cell phone showed as thirty-four minutes, all I could find were ponds of koi after koi. Scales of white, orange and gold refracting the lights from the skyscrapers above. I contemplated taking the Omikuji home to translate the message when I had access to the Internet, but I was put off by the sounds of a miserable salaryman being sick next to an urban shrine. The torrents of cascading vomit made up my mind. I gently tossed the piece of paper into one of the ponds, the words of my fate consigned to the depths of the koi.

A little luck, uncertain luck, certain disaster.

Like the spontaneous pool of the salaryman's vomit, some things that occur in the city at night are better left unknown to the light of ensuing morning.

MANGA KISSA I

*****

When I felt utterly defeated, which was most days, I would walk through the faint intimation of rain and lights to a manga kissa – basically a comic book café where you could sleep, binge watch anime on prescription drugs and buy snacks and assorted beverages. You could rent a pod for like the equivalent of $12 for 3-5 hours or you could shell out a few more peas for a longer stint in the booth at some places. They were cheaper than a capsule hotel and I found the melancholic vibes more to my liking. Manga kissa were a moment out of life and people here felt like they could basically come home to them. They were more of a home than the inhabitant's shoebox homes. The second manga kissa. The third. The fourth. They were all seemingly the same age and looked exactly the same.

To put things bluntly: visiting a manga kissa was like a little hug. Or the sound of a 2814 song from that album with the cult vaporwave cover. When you entered and slipped into the comfortable confines of the booth, everything was that sound. Silence drowned out by an inner monologue of emotive, droning ambient.

It was here at the manga kissa that I was introduced to the Japanese drink Doumoshi. If you're a fan of mochi and mochi-based drinks, then you might want to try this fucker. It's made with egg noodles that have been soaked with soy sauce and rice syrup, then coated in white rice flour and flavoured to taste. When you stir it, it gets really sticky and gloopy, which is exactly what you want when you're using this drink to cleanse the muscles around your chest, which is supposedly what it does. While I was at the manga kissa, I often had a weird desire to 'eat' a ton of Doumoshi and drink a ton of Bikkle, a more common Japanese yoghurt-based drink. I loved my anime combined with drink so much that, every Friday night, I'd go devour a combo of both in the micro-library at Kita-senpai's manga kissa across the street from my apartment.

The advertisement for Duomoshi was amazing too. It had dogs with sunglasses in it. And everything on screen was a melted horizon blue. I would mention the advertisement to people at work and strongly recommend to my colleagues they try Duomoshi. I would say shit like: "if you don't want to get angry when you're drinking something, drink Duomoshi." I would give them information about its chest cleansing capabilities and tell them to try it and not feel bad about getting angry. If they wanted to try it, it only cost a little to get some at a local convenience store. I would pick up a bottle on my way home from work to accompany a savoury snack like mentaiko Cheetos or unagi flavoured potato chips. It was strange how little people knew about it though, even Japanese people familiar with all the seasonal food and beverage products were unaware of its existence. Whenever someone tried it based on my recommendation, they would report back to me and state they didn't 'get' the taste. I never knew if they meant the taste or just 'the taste,' you know?

Kissa just means café. But whenever I think of the word it evokes a memorable scene from this anime that I binge watched on Valium one night. The anime's main character Kirito is having sex with a girl who is not his love interest at first sight, but she thinks she is. She insistently tells him that they fell in love at first sight, but he tells her she's gone all wrong. He continues to engage with her though and she becomes aroused. He then continues to say he doesn't love her and reveals he wants to give her a 'Kissa moment' as a parting gift. To do this he takes out his penis and says, "Kissa! Kissa!" Then they make love for several minutes before it cuts to a scene where Kirito is lost on a deserted beach screaming her name. Then the episode kind of drifts to an end.

*****

I don't know where else to go, so I'm here again at the manga kissa. Evangelion is on the screen, prescription pills are in my pocket and I'm sipping an ice cold Doumoshi that sits at the compact table by my side. I pick up the glass vessel containing the Duomoshi. I observe it carefully. Let my mouth brim with the Japanese drink Duomoshi. Let it flow with that gluggy, syrupy goodness. It's the genuine taste of a quality manga kissa. It's the taste of a perfect man's tongue, filled with the sensual essence of art itself.

Sometimes it is served fermented with sugar or honey. Sometimes it is just served raw. As a rule, as it ages, you are left with a mellower taste, with less bitterness. The yuzu version is particularly to my liking. With such an iconic, uniquely-shaped name, I can't even really describe it without losing my train of thought. What I know for sure is that the quality of it is superior to anything you can get from other beverage sources. To be that far apart from other drinks seems almost impossible, but when you consume it, it is incredible.

"Here we have a drink," I say out loud, as if I am narrating the product's horizon blue advertisement.

"On the outside it looks similar to the old Japanese coffee, except that the syrup is different. The colour of the syrup should also match the rest of the drink in terms of overall consistency. I always try to do my best to consume this drink in the style that Japanese men love, where they say that the syrup is the colour of their heart."

But of course, the colours of each heart are definitively different. They cannot be the same for everyone. So, I've had to be content that there's definitely different people and no doubt different styles of men. I take a slurp of the gooey contents of the Duomoshi. I drop a couple of Valium and select an anime at random. Tell me, where else would I rather be?

MORNING RITUAL

*****

I used to take milk with my coffee until I moved here. It just got too difficult to ask for 'a little' milk in another language. Even my hand gestures were mistaken. My thumb and index finger lifted ever so slightly to create clear separation of a couple of centimetres of gaseous matter, my face wincing to convey exactly how much milk I required to get the balance right. Trying my best to mimic the conservative politeness of whomever was serving me.

But it never worked. There was inevitably a question I did not understand which followed my unclear request, or they would nod in understanding and proceed to fill the cup with what felt like litres and litres of milk. These exchanges resulted in pure shame and embarrassment in me. Why could I not be smart enough or motivated enough to learn how to ask for just 'a little' milk in another language? The rage and hopelessness felt like what I imagined a teenage girl late to puberty felt as her friends were all busy growing boobs and talking about their periods. Alone and constantly wondering 'Why me? Why can't I be like all the others?'

I would practice at home in the mirror, trying the phrase out, letting the poorly pronounced syllables float in the dead air of my apartment. I would try it with the hand gestures, I would try it without the hand gestures. I would do things like alter my posture to see if it made a difference in my delivery. I would experiment with a terse delivery, then I would try it nonchalantly. I would go on until I was utterly disorientated and defeated, unable to even remember if I had the sounds in the right order. These sessions generally culminated in me pulling various 'extreme' facial expressions in the mirror without delivering the imperfect milk mantra any further. The face staring back at me like a burnt-out husk, exhausted and expended of all energy after such a gruelling interrogation.

Sure enough, the next morning at the café attached to the lobby of the hotel adjacent to my apartment complex I would botch my next attempt to ask for only 'a little' milk.

Even if the café staff members got it right based off my indecipherable request, I had no confidence I would be able to convey to them that yes, this is what I wanted for now and the future. 'Please, oh please, just like this every time' I would plead with my tedious eyes. Though this would not do the trick. Nothing would do the trick's trick. And another linguistic battle would ensue. The thoughts of the subsequent steps required to cement my request in their minds, even if they finally served up what I was trying to articulate, was enough to deter me from any further dishonourable attempts.

My path was decided. I would migrate to black coffee. 'Espresso', a common enough nomenclature in these parts, that even my horrible communication skills could be understood when blurting it out in front of the register.

Now, I don't even think twice when ordering my caffeinated beverage of choice. The vestiges of just 'a little' milk atrophying to a point that the neurons holding this information have become ostracised from the other parts of my brain. Like an orbiting moon sucked into a blackhole.

So, the word 'espresso' and this hotel lobby café became my Japanese morning ritual. It was one day while ordering my usual coffee at this café attached to the hotel lobby that I first encountered Katie. She was soon to be my oxygen. The lemon-yellow sweater she wore burning a hole in my memory.

RELATIONSHIP

* * * * *

This is how I met Katie. I was sitting at my morning coffee place. I observed her as she approached the counter. Her lemon-yellow sweater flattened all my feelings into one smooth integer for her soul. She stopped to pick up a tray from a neatly stacked pile, collecting an almond croissant and a small breaded ball that resembled a tightly coiled brown sponge. Kind of like a miniature armadillo. I didn't know the name of this treat, so I just called it the 'armadillo sponge.' After a moment's hesitation, as though she may have forgotten something, she quickly turned and proceeded to the queue for the register. I was seated at a small table near the window, sipping my too hot coffee, wondering whether she resided in the neighbourhood or if she was merely passing through for a job interview at a nearby English school. It was odd to see a foreigner on the fringes I chose to cling. It was clear she was not out this far for tourist purposes. Only odd men of esoteric leisure like me came out this far. Strange individuals that wanted to seek out the mirror world equivalent of satellite suburban fringe life. Places full of twenty-first century anonymity and alienation. Ironically, the very thing I was escaping.

When she reached the front of the line, I was startled by the sound of her voice as she uttered the word 'espresso.' I remember thinking that perhaps she too had 'a little' milk dilemma. As she waited patiently for her coffee, I tried to think of plausible ways I could engage her in conversation. Should I try out some witty material if she walked my way? Perhaps just a beaming smile would do?

'Beaming' I thought, somewhat creepily.

Then there was always the 'pose a faux question you don't really want an answer to method.'

"Hey, I just moved into the area, where do you find the best replica of a hamburger?" Or some utter garbage. Would that shit even work?

I didn't need to worry though, as upon receiving her coffee and depositing it on her tray, she walked directly over to my table and sat down as if it was the most natural thing in the world.

"I prefer blueberry croissants to almond croissants ordinarily, but they're consistently all out here." She said as if we were resuming a conversation from earlier in the morning. Those were her first words.

"Um. That's a shame." I said, staring at her.

It was all I could think of to say after this unexpected turn of events, my lengthy inner monologue regarding potential topics of conversation utterly eclipsed.

"I had a fall this morning." She went on in a familiar tone.

"The kind of fall only an attractive girl carrying a number of upmarket shopping bags on a train station escalator can have. You know, awkward but still graceful."

An awkward, graceful fall? Upmarket shopping bags? What bizarre world had I unwittingly entered? I couldn't comprehend what the fuck she was talking about. Later, Katie would tell me this was her 'Murakami' test for guys she liked upon first glance. I guess I passed as a 'Murakami' guy.

At the time, I had no response to this. I remember just staring at her tasteful yet artificial blonde hair shimmering in the morning sun. It smelled amazing. I kept thinking that this is how babies must smell to their parents during tender moments or some other such cliché detritus.

I recall she took a bite of her croissant and made a face like she had lost something important. She then made a little giggling sound as she reached for her coffee.

"You too?" she said, gesturing towards my cup.

"Espresso. It's the only thing I know how to order," I said.

She looked at my face closely at this point, examining it, seeing if it was real. Seeing if there was any truth below the filmy façade of flesh and bones. She tells me that I was intently examining the worn edge of the table at this stage. Examining imperceptible blemishes to the unobservant eye. Distracted by the ecstasies of inscrutable marks and blurred lines.

"You can try some of this, since you can't order anything else." She said, pushing forward the tray with the croissant and the weird breaded sponge ball.

I mechanically tore off a portion of the breaded sponge thing and popped it into my mouth. It was too sweet for my tastes, but inoffensive enough. The texture was slightly gelatinous, the inside extremely chewy despite its soft outward appearance. It reminded me of a deep-sea organism.

"What are you doing here?" I asked her.

"I drift in and out of places. Places where I'm needed."

Fucking Murakami. The riddles. The hints. How could someone speak to a person like this in real life? I soon found out it was only upon first meeting she resorted to this unnecessary foreplay.

"What kind of places?" I played along, did the Murakami thing.

"Places where sound is faint, colours are muted and people are what they pretend to be."

I probably should have walked at that point, but I didn't, couldn't.

Following this odd exchange, Katie animatedly poked me firmly in the ribs. Shocked, I still can feel the moment when I hastily recoiled. What kind of creature was this?

She smirked and went on unperturbed, returning to more familiar matters.

"Well, I do enjoy the coffee here, but I best be going to my next appointment."

I still don't know if she was implying that we had one, whatever this moment was. This first sighting.

I don't know if this part of the memory is exactly right, but the way it plays in my mind is: she hurriedly stood up, smoothed her clothing and passed a small nondescript item to me. I felt the weight of the item and opened my palm to reveal a book of matches. I didn't even know people still used them. The only thing on the packet was a Line ID and a picture of an eye with a lightning bolt streaming tears. The world blurred a bit, and I remember looking down and noticed Katie's coffee was drained. The baked goods had been polished off and a tiny portion of neat crumbs remained.

I turned to face the exit and could see her well-proportioned figure confidently receding. The image of her decreasing body size from my perspective like a sunken object steadily obscured by hazy water. This was Katie.

NARA, JAPAN I

*****

I started seeing Katie after this. Like 'romantically' I suppose you would call it. It turned out she lived in a virtually identical apartment complex down the road from Damien's source. Katie was the first to introduce me to Nara, Japan and the throngs of deer residing in the park. One day, she decided to take the train on a whim. She asked me if I would like to tag along.

"It's only forty-five minutes and you don't need to change lines," she told me.

Her voice sounded strange and unfamiliar, like she was entombed in a Turkish bath house as I listened to her in real-time on my pre-paid flip phone – she told me it was the cheapest model available. Apparently, they didn't even sell them anymore.

We met at a large metropolitan station mid-morning. I don't recall the name. All one and the same. I drank a can of iced coffee from a hole-in-the-wall convenience store while I waited. People walked by – faceless, nameless people. Some people did wear expressions where the faces should have been, but the expressions were smudged, deliberately obscuring whatever intent lay underneath.

Others wore ill-fitting masks, smeared or pasted on the skin and left to dry, like split eggplants basted with miso paste left in the intense summer sun. Their features slowly congealing into a new entity – like a stop-motion leaking of time. A select few were unable to hide. Their true colours on display for all to see. These misfits were ceremoniously ignored and consistently seen as 'not fit for society,' rejected by the orderly imposters that were approved to move seamlessly through the interzone. I ensured I played my role and did not bring attention to these non-beings. Their presence always felt though, like a hard lump in the throat that prevents one from swallowing.

Amongst these proud yet confused tribes of twenty-first century ideals, she emerged from the chittering crowds.

"Do you need a ticket?"

"Icoca."

"What?"

"Icoca," I repeated softly, a lack of confidence setting in, uncertain of my pronunciation of this alien set of letters bundled together. Not an acronym, nor part of any 'real' language – a word one shouldn't utter aloud. A word best left for the 'void'.

"Icoca," I said again with more certainty, in a tone that belied my bemusement at the sequence of verbal utterances we were currently exchanging. I held up the blue-silver plastic travel card in recognition, gesturing to the cartoon penguin emblazoned on the surface.

"Oh," Katie said. "Icoca."

"I thought it was called something else." She added after some time had passed.

*****

On the train, we talked about trivial things – different flavoured mints, why we found people who were fascinated by cars utterly incomprehensible, her extremely overweight cat that I met last time I was at her 1DK apartment. The cat's name was Yukio Mishima, named after the Japanese writer and I was particularly fascinated by it. I recalled observing it as it sat on the compact fold-out sofa, attempting to lick its genitals, yet failing to do so successfully due to the girth that inhibited its daily cat rituals.

While observing it during this miserable moment, I remembered that I couldn't stop thinking if I traded souls with the cat, perhaps the first, and best thing, I could do was to commit seppuku in honour of its given name. Observing this fat cat at her apartment made me feel how sad and absurd the world was. To be an overweight cat owned by a foreigner in Japan.

But the cat didn't know any of this. It couldn't comprehend concepts like alienation or international travel or boredom. It just was. Not fathoming how a series of intertwined events could lead to its current bed of roses. Despite the relatively carefree life it led (weight issues aside) it had no autonomy, nor freedom, to make its own choices. Everything it had, or did, dictated by the decisions of another. All outcomes pre-determined.

I often wondered if it could understand concepts like envy or jealousy would it yearn to be transformed into a more agile feline, like the ones I often viewed from the balcony of my apartment? The indistinct forms of black and mottled grey sitting patiently next to disorderly makeshift gardens at dusk, waiting for the next meme of their lives to unfold. Or would Yukio Mishima choose to stay as he was, content in his hedonistic ways, satisfied with the food and shelter provided so 'generously,' willing to make this trade-off for any real ability to clean himself efficiently?

*****

Shogeki.

"Touch your pass again." She says as she attempts to exit the station.

Touching my pass again to the sensor at the station gates, I am greeted by the intermittent flashing of red and white lights indicating there is a problem with my fare. The red and white lights are not menacing – more thoughtful, like a reminder to complete some semi-important task. An embellished mash-up of hieroglyphs encoded within. A semiotic fugue only introduced upon the first touch, then, recurring frequently throughout the duration of the composition, somewhat soothing in tone. Silently, without thinking, I turn my body on a 180-degree angle and withdraw from the erect barrier to accommodate the mass of my virtually empty shoulder bag, automatically shuttling myself to the ticket machine nearby.

The mixture of the heat in the underground concrete space and the slight acrid smell of chemicals mollify as I glide effortlessly to a set of four adjoined somewhat chunky ticket machines. I mechanically insert my shiny blue-silver pass and deposit the change needed to gain access to the human world above, to legally comply with my obligation as a public transport using person. I find it astounding that a machine of such girth is necessary to complete this menial task. Like one of those super computers from the '60s you see images of on Wikipedia with a cacophony of jovial professors standing around, beaming smiles as they consider the previously unfathomable possibilities of a thousand-kilogram machine playing a game of chess. A complete contrast to the recently recharged touchless smart card that I hold in my palm.

Katie is waiting for me patiently at the gates. Not being able to tell how much time has passed, I touch my pass to the sensor once more, a feeling of dread setting in, my thought pattern 'Kafkaesque' as I ponder what I can possibly do if my card is rejected again – no man can 'afford' to be thrown back into the throes of the red and white semiotic abyss. The sensor beams green though, a chime dings, the barriers stand to attention and part. Free passage to the very different hemisphere on the other side awaits.

As I ascend the stairs with her, hand in hand, all I can feel is something vacant settle in.

*****

On the surface, everything is different. A redolent hush hangs over the terrain despite the fact we have emerged in an area populated by shops, restaurants and other layered urban density. It is uncannily silent. Walking through this stillness, it is oddly intimate. The atmosphere is deeply delicate and personal despite neither of us ever having been here before.

There are vehicles parked, but virtually none that are moving. Squashed, stationary little things. Like baby beetles rooted to the spot on the floor as a home owner goes about their daily cleaning.

Trying to avoid movement unless absolutely necessary. When one car does move, it does so almost imperceptibly, with a level of methodical politeness. Like it needs to move with purpose but cannot bring itself to breach the stillness of the surrounding air.

We walked past a bakery, a restaurant serving curry, a shop selling unidentified sweets lined up in matte silver trays. Aimless meanderings. Were we lost in the looping peculiar geometrical pockets of urban Japan?

"You just follow this road for like ten minutes, then you will see them."

I mulled over the possibility that Katie could read minds. Only select minds though, with people she has certain bonds with. I imagined her explaining the ability of her powers in painstaking detail to me, like we were in some Hollywood movie. A heart wrenching scene where the audience truly understood the pain of her burden, but also felt touched due to the connection between the two main characters.

"Can you read minds?" I responded, unsure if I verbalised this or said it internally.

She shrugged and laughed, affirming that my response was audible.

"I can only read the minds of people I have a special bond with." She said, squeezing my hand.

I nodded absently. Returned the squeeze quietly.

"Like in the movies." I said to no one in particular.

*****

We walked the rest of the way without saying anything, neither of us wanting to disrupt the relaxed yet disorderly environment we found ourselves in. An environment free of constraints – purely abstract in nature. Only certain sounds were permitted and selected from a specific criterion. The intermittent beeping of the pedestrian crossing signs at traffic lights, worn plastic sandals gently scraping the pavement as elderly people slowly moved from Point A to Point B and various other points they were destined to flow, the swish of cheap business pants worn by salarymen as they pedalled their nondescript bicycles.

Open secrets only shared if you listen closely and follow the flow.

*****

The first deer we see are unremarkable. They nestle together next to a pagoda on the gravel path, grazing in the shadow of a nearby tree. Their bodies don't move at all upon noticing our presence. No perceptible difference in their breathing, the rise and fall of their subtle diaphragms relaxed and constant. The only discernible change in their appearance the position of their glistening black eyeballs, ever so slightly moving in the direction we approach from.

I don't know what I expected. Maybe something from Bambi. Or maybe that they would flee immediately once they saw us coming down the path. But it made sense that they stayed in place. After all they were used to people coming here, had evolved to incorporate interaction with these strange creatures that co-existed with them. The percentage that we were one of the select few humans to 'go rogue' was not worth the energy expended to migrate from their comfortable position under the tree.

One thing that really shocked me was that the deer would stand still, transfixed by people holding biscuits. Like passengers on a journey to another level of consciousness. Something bright and luminesce behind the sclera of their eyes, hidden from view, but on the surface, merely a vacant gaze reflecting the gifts of the banal consumer culture they somehow found themselves in.

At a nearby vending machine, I decide to purchase a cold green tea. What did the deer stare at before the 'biscuit epoch?' What held their semi-detached gaze before this point in time? To consider this is a lesson in temporality. The cool tea soothes my throat. I sip it while watching the deer compete for snacks only metres away.

*****

There were signs around that indicated the deer could become aggressive. Signs that showed little speech bubbles that came from the outline of a cartoon deer that read 'butt' and 'kick' and 'stomp' and 'bite' and so on. I had heard from a friend that the deer would only get physical with small children, like a bully that only beats on the tiny, the weak, the pathetic.

There was, however, a depiction of an elderly lady being 'butted' on the sign. I wondered how that scene would play out in real life. What would happen in the aftermath? Would anyone come to the old woman's aid? Or would passers-by merely direct her attention to the sign, reiterating the disclaimer to the contract she had unwittingly entered.

Caveat emptor.

Buyer beware.

"Would you bring your grandmother here?" I asked Katie.

"Would I bring my grandmother here? Would I like to bring her here and show her round, is that what you mean?"

"Yeah, bring her here and show her around."

"Hmmm. Could I bring my grandfather too?"

"Um. I guess."

"I guess so then... If I didn't have to endure a ten-hour flight with them to get here."

"If they could be teleported, then you would take them here, to see the deer in the park?"

"Yeah, if they were teleported. I would."

She wanted to continue, but then hesitated, something tugged at her inside as she observed the surrounding vegetation with renewed scrutiny.

"But the only thing is... I think my grandfather hates Japan. Like, he's not fond of it. Because of memories of the war," she went on.

"I'm pretty confident he has a strong distaste for it. For the people."

"And my grandmother, I think she would be indifferent. More tolerant, but like, I don't think she could adapt to the food. She would be shocked that people don't eat the things she thinks they eat. I mean, her preconception of what a Japanese person eats."

"What does she think they eat?" I said.

"Hmmm. I guess the narrow worldview she possesses would probably point to, like, what's served at an 'Asian' take away joint? Greasy pork dyed with food colouring, noodles drenched in sweetened soy sauce – that sort of thing. I think the shock of seeing them eat different things – some foreign, some familiar – like sandwiches for instance would be too much for her."

Hearing Katie speak so candidly about her grandparents, I wondered whether I had preconceptions about different demographics – different ethnicities and subcultures. No matter how 'educated' I was, I'm sure I did. Like, if I took a flight to Yemen tomorrow, a country I knew nothing about, what would I be thinking on the flight? How would I 'prepare?' What kind of scenes of an average life in Yemen would my mind be able to muster?

"Maybe, you could download a video of a perspective of someone walking through Nara, Japan and then play it while your grandparents walk on the treadmill, like those newer treadmills with the built-in touch screens they have at the gym." I said.

"Oh yeah, they seem more user-friendly. I saw one of those for Yosemite National Park and Gastown in Vancouver once. The people in the videos all looked so discontent. I wonder what the people here would look like on the walking video?" She said.

I continued observing the deer.

"Probably indifferent." I said staring fixedly on a tenuous shrub in the near distance. I looked at Katie's shoes as the surrounding cicadas warned my heart with their cry. The liquid green tea in my bottle was slowly becoming warm.

ETHEREAL NIGHTS

* * * * *

We are walking through city night. Light envelops us in comfortable snow noise as Katie grips my hand. The note of every emotion's little chord plays across the breadth of our faces. We will stop at nothing to go to these lengths. Laughter and hints of opalescent smiles, we imbibe dirty martinis for 500 Yen. Cocktails for a coin almost equal to her perfect face. We spend our time loving, losing, crushing. This night will raw me, and not just because of the MDMA.

Karaoke in a liminal dog-box upstairs. Drinking and limitlessly spilling our guts into the microphone, into each other, all for 2000 Yen. The cosmic desire of split lips tuning the rhythm of our star-mangled hearts. An ever-presence of sultry muscles spasming in the dark. Her lips and breath shimmering like layers of rhodochrosite. In these throes, she is my plastic girl. Pink, shiny, feathered – the cherry pit in the throes of cascading ultrablast.

Slipping, grasping, clutching black taxi door handles, we fall into a heap of neon purple mud. Katie's oxygen infiltrated with glitter, every minute breath tracing the outline of a gossamer lung. Streams of light slide by glass in the hues of an openheart. The driver's white gloves glowburn – our retinas bathed in milky white. Halo of sharded skyscrapers drip in and out of vision as our mood thaws. Katie's head meets my shoulder, her feelings perched like a tiny bird, comfortable enough to die. Hieroglyphic signs pulsate like iridescent coral marbles. Content enough to call this comet home.

INTERIOR DESIGN

* * * * *

Katie invited me over for pizza. The weather was beginning to get cold. That awkward time of year in Japan when the air conditioning was still automatically set to the maximum, but the temperature outside was already mild. You had to wear layers and layers of clothes for about two weeks on the public transport system until the people that ran it finally caught up to understand what everyone already knew – that air conditioning was entirely unnecessary in this climate. The frigid air was just another burden for commuters to deal with, delicately crushing their already pummelled sentiments into a fine paste. The same thing would happen when the winter months came around and turned into spring, only in reverse. This was decidedly worse, as you were trapped in a carriage with the heating cranked up all the way, meanwhile the weather outside was warm enough to roam around in a T-shirt.

Her apartment complex was clean, but not new. The garish austerity of post-bubble '90s Japan written all over its façade. Those weird micro tiles covering the external walls. An inoffensive light-brown the colour of choice. To get to the entrance, you clamoured past mountains of trash separated into myriad sections of small to medium sized garbage bags in a way only the Japanese can do. Each plastic category seemingly getting its own unique position in the queue for collection by a specialised service designated for that specific type of plastic. It was supposed to make things more orderly, but from what I could gather it just complicated matters. Even here there would be people that didn't follow the rules – out of discontent, out of laziness, out of rebellion, out of boredom. Inevitably, you would observe a stray noodle cup or Styrofoam container still smeared with congealed mayonnaise lying desperate and alone. These items were treated as pariahs, dismal oddities that continued to contribute to the putrid area surrounding the polychromatic dumpster. Forever untouched by the filthy gloves of the garbagemen due to their position outside any appropriate category.

Disorder in order.

Function over form.

It was all enough to make people go a little insane. And they certainly did. The shrill cries of smashed white-collar salarymen often heard echoing through the cavernous depths of the metro stations. Muted sounds of deranged and alienated foot soldiers finally giving in.

Past what I endearingly termed 'trash cove,' there was a double door you could enter with a code or a key. I always used the code. I wasn't even sure if Katie had a key. Once you input the code, only one of the double doors opened. It was large enough to fit a bicycle through or alternatively walk through holding about four bags of groceries without turning sideways. In the relatively large atrium, there were nondescript mailboxes and an aged umbrella stand beyond which lied one of the smallest elevators I've ever seen. Whenever I travelled in it, I thought of insects trapped in a lantern, the beating of tiny wings imprisoned in milky light. Once inside the elevator, it was reminiscent of times during my childhood when I would hide in my grandmother's cupboard. Stuffy yet reassuring. Sharing it with strangers was an exhilarating experience. It always amazed me when individual living organisms were put in a position of such proximity without any sensory exchange. The profound absence of any intimacy or violence in these circumstances resounded strongly with me. What kind of animals had we become? A species that had evolved to a point of mechanical numbness? Emotional instincts eroded by banal domesticity. To express these emotions, to act on these instincts like the busted foot soldiers in the metro stations, one would be forbidden.

Her apartment was on the fifth floor. Oddly, it was the only one on the floor, the rest of the floor taken up by something unknown. A zone cordoned off by an L-shaped wall, whatever lay beneath an eternal secret. It could have just been blank space, it could have been insulation, or it could have been something essential to the functionality and well-being of the building (certainly observing the position where this void was located, there was nothing discernibly different from the outside). There was a fire door that seemingly led into this indeterminate space, however, it was always locked. We had never seen anyone use it, in fact we had never observed any other human beings on the floor at all. Which did make sense, given there was only one apartment on the level. To get to Katie's apartment, you walked down this awkward mini-corridor. I'm not even sure why this precursor to her front door existed. Seemed like a waste, like they had missed a beat, by not designing the level so the tiny elevator opened directly in line with the door to the apartment. Save the extra couple of tatami's of surface area for the interior of the apartment. These were the kinds of thoughts that wandered through my head all the time – meaningless, trivial, abstract. Necessary work in getting to points that were more meaningful. Distractions that served the higher purpose of letting me float on by.

“Interior design.” I said aloud, to see how it felt.

Saying this out loud in such a space felt unnerving. The sound of the words made me contemplate destroying myself. Covering the gaps in my life so they would be bereft of air – blocking the gaps, obscuring the gaps, forgetting the gaps were there to begin with.

She opened the door before the requirement of knocking. The door swung freely and nearly crushed her due to a combination of the forceful manner in which she opened it and her complete lack of balance holding the heavy door. This was her signature style when it came to everything – I termed it ‘orderly awkward.’ Her often uncoordinated motor skills having a finely tuned synchronicity. Her coordination on par with a regular person, but her equilibrium completely off.

She wore a white top that said ‘YUKIO MISHIMA’ in black letters above the picture of a black cartoon cat printed on the white background. She told me after some time, this is actually how she came to name her fat cat. He was not just named after the famous author, but also a cheap misshapen T-shirt. The cut of the T-shirt looked like it would be confusing to store. You couldn’t really hang it up. Nor would it fold properly to be stored in a drawer. It seemed like a garment best placed on a chair or a rug on the floor – its free-flowing design marketed to suit a messy chic lifestyle in which the owner ironically pretends they’re a character in a TV show from the mid ‘90s. Daria came to mind for some reason. Did people still use furniture to temporarily hang their clothes?

Katie’s apartment smelled nice. Like she just showered and washed her clothes in one swift hit before I came over. The atmosphere resembled an amniotic bath. It was enough to make my insides runny like a cracked egg.

"This is it. This is all I have," she said as I looked around her room.

This was a running joke whenever I came to her apartment. As I stepped inside, she would make a sweeping, expansive gesture with her arm inviting me to panoramically view the contents of her apartment. My eyes would normally fall on Yukio Mishima, his eyes locked on a mark in front of him, deeply concentrating on licking the insides of his nether-world as he loved to do.

"I ordered a flavour we haven't tried." Katie said.

"No avocado this time?"

"Weirder."

Japan seemed to create totally insane flavour combinations for just about every food. The pizza was on another level though. We would order from Domino's because they had an English version of the menu and website. They also delivered post-haste. The pizza toppings ranged from avocado-shrimp to potato with 'sizzling hot' mayo. They didn't taste that bad once you got over the initial shock. Katie and I would normally order one 'standard' pizza, a mainstay that we would have back in our respective home countries of America and Australia, and a 'freaked out' pizza, which basically meant we picked out the most absurd flying disk on the menu. Pickled squid with wasabi sauce, Korean BBQ and prawn, chashu ramen pork... You name it, they had it, we fucking tried it.

When the delivery dude arrived, politely nodding and bowing as the delivery dudes here do, I opened both boxes to find out what was on the menu for the evening. I looked at the 'standard' pizza – it was pepperoni. I looked at the 'freaked out' pizza – it looked like tuna and corn, with a holy hellscape of mayo drizzled all over its surface. I checked the receipt on top of the box, it said 'Tuna Mild.'

"What do you think?" Katie said.

I didn't know how to feel about the name. What was mild about tuna and corn on top of a pizza? It kind of had a nice calming effect on my brain though, the 'mild' part.

"I think they designed the name for people who have a lot of panic attacks." I said

Katie laughed. "Yeah, totally mild."

We ate the pizza harmoniously and watched weird shows we couldn't understand on TV. We slammed down some lime-flavoured chuhai she had lying around, both of us thoroughly satisfied it was the 'super strong' style at 12%. We played drinking games to the TV shows flickering past. We created abstract rules based on the content of the shows and accompanying advertisements. Whenever the Softbank dog made an appearance, the last person to scream out "Softbanku!" would have to chug the rest of their tall boy. It was a recipe for disastrous fun. On the third drinking game, with the pizza quietly demolished, Katie drastically subsided, her unsuspecting body declining to a level of unconsciousness on the small sofa. Looking around the apartment while she slept, thinking of her panoramic hand gesture, I realised at that moment how happy I was. The fuzz of the peach I had been searching for was finally kissing my skin. I laid back on the sofa. My body and mind entirely settled as I watched Yukio Mishima nibble at the remains of the 'tuna mild' pizza, the draft of warm winds surrounding us more beautiful than silence.

EMPLOYMENT II

*****

I first met Glenn when I applied for a job at an 'after hours' English school. I wasn't getting booked at Dainichi as I was still in sore need of a gimmick. I needed to make some more money, craved it bad like a hole-in-the-head. The school was located in the equivalent of a lower-class suburb in an Anglified country. It was an area full of Japanese families who didn't know anything of the world outside variety shows, baseball mascots and the seasonal products available at differing convenience store franchises. Their accents were all rough as shit and they would spend hours a day talking about their favourite takoyaki sauce and toppings. Their kids would have standard pumpkin-pie headed bowl cuts and most of the mothers worked the local snack bar, their role to whisper sweet nothings to down and out salarymen whose wives would no longer touch them while they drank themselves to death. The boys would all skip class and head to the local 100 Yen shop to buy esoteric ephemera used to catch various insects. Kobo Abe once said that kids who collect insects often have an Oedipus complex. It was certainly common knowledge these kids slept in the same bed as their mothers until they were teenagers. Their inability to afford more than a basic 1DK apartment meant they didn't really have a choice. The fathers all had course yet mushy faces like the texture of a trodden on fast-food paper bag. They were totally uncouth and dutifully beat the shit out of their spouses and children, eating fermented squid guts as they guzzled down chuhai and happoshu, that cheap Japanese beer that isn't actually beer. It was all kind of not what an average foreigner came to think of when they thought of Japan. Glenn and I both loved it though, were drawn to it. The scum, the filth, the hustling. To us, it proved that anywhere in the world is like everywhere else. Regardless of a nation's outward perception, there were always people simmering below the surface trying their best to get by. Attempting to fumble through their meaningless existence. Given our penchant for grime, Glenn and I instantly hit it off. Our preference for scungy Japanese punk music venues and the consumption of offal on sticks at local standing bars amongst the sweating masses were joys we shared. It goes without saying that these joys were not shared by most other foreigners who chose to visit Japan. Glenn and I were not like other people though, we had fully forfeited the Western wonders of the world: responsibility, debt, the family SUV. These were not 'luxuries' our tiny hearts could handle.

At the 'after hours' English school, Glenn and I would attempt to teach these quasi English texts to small-minded kids from the neighbourhood while they muttered things about smut and wanting to kill us in the hushed tones of their rugged native Kansai dialect. Most times we just played games though. The smaller kids in particular were great. There was this one kid named Rikito who would always pretend to be a dog and run around in circles until he fell down, perspiring profusely. Rikito was awesome. He would constantly draw pictures of steaming shit instead of copying the English words off the whiteboard. He was ecstatic when upon 'catching him' in the act of drawing excrement, instead of lambasting him like the other teachers, I casually pointed at the image and taught him the English word poo. From that day on, the boys in the class would all shout the word out until their lungs were sore, not satisfied until the middle-aged female owner of the school would come in to settle things down. We all had a good laugh.

When Glenn gave me the job at the school, I replaced this other Western teacher named Clint. Clint was fluent in Japanese. He was also a brazen alcoholic. His face was covered in burst blood vessels and his hands were constantly shaking during class. Glenn told me that he got fired because his breath constantly reeked of cheap Japanese whiskey. Glenn said Clint would order unruly kids to sit underneath the sink where they washed their hands and referred to them as cockroaches in his fluent Japanese. Glenn felt sorry for Clint and said that his behaviour was acceptable in Korea, where he taught English before he came to Japan. It was sad to see Clint's eyes water at the culmination of his last lesson when he officially handed the teaching reigns over to me. I won't forget how he stared into space and pondered whether he should go back to Korea or to the United Kingdom, where he was born. It was obvious too much time had passed and there was nothing left for him in these places. He didn't belong. However, it was clear that nothing was available for him in Japan besides liquor-soaked nights seated forlornly at the local snack bar. After 13 years of sameness, it had grown old, even for someone like Clint. The expat dream was dead.

'After hours' classes generally ran from 5:30pm – 9:30pm. After class, Glenn and I would swing by the local convenience store and grab a couple of tall cans of beer or chuhai on our bicycles. We would ride to an abandoned construction site next to the metro station and sneak in through the chain-link fence. We would climb up onto this oddly shaped embankment so we would be at eye level of one overhead trainline and beneath another. We would talk about how our lives were fucked, about philosophy, about music, about all kinds of shit in this setting. Nestled amongst the overlapping tracks, the mood was conducive to honest outpourings, you know, for forgiveness. One night in this location, Glenn told me that he lived in Japan for many years and was engaged to marry a local girl who he described as "really Japanese. Like, real traditional," and then he freaked out and had a panic attack when he was playing guitar maybe ~10 days before the wedding. He immediately booked a plane ticket back to his home state of Alberta, Canada and skipped out on the whole thing. Back home, he tried to re-assimilate, but like Clint, too much time had passed. There was nothing for him in rural Alberta anymore. Glenn tried to get jobs, but he couldn't hold any of them. He said the final straw was when he was working as a truck driver and he was constantly abused by his co-workers who called him a faggot because of his long, luxurious Rockstar hair. He quit that day, then went to a party. At the party he realised that all the people in attendance had not changed in seven years, they were still talking about the same stuff they did years ago. Now the only difference was they had jobs, mortgages, more expensive television sets, kids – things Glenn had no desire for. Glenn decided that he would either kill himself that night or buy a ticket to come back to Japan. Glenn tried the first, but as his colleague at the truck company eluded to, he wasn't man enough to complete the job. So, he grudgingly purchased a one-way fare back to the land of the rising sun. Upon his return he almost annihilated his inner Self in a catastrophic tour of drinking and drugs for the first week, until one of his Japanese guitar mentors found him face down in a karaoke joint toilet where he called an on-the-spot intervention. He said all that he remembers of the moment is looking at the collar of his most-loved Spacemen 3 T-shirt. The trippy logo covered in flecks of vomit that intermingled with the shirt's design. He doesn't recall the words of his mentor, but that band logo covered in vomit was poignant enough on its own to act as the epiphany he needed.

This realisation made Glenn re-contact his former fiancée, and he told me they were in discussions about repairing their relationship. Glenn said that her parents would never forgive him. Glenn said that when he re-emerged into her life, he summoned the courage to pay a visit to her family home to apologise and reconcile with her extended family. On this visit, her father openly asked him in front of all in attendance how much money Glenn made as an English teacher and musician. When Glenn provided the paltry sum in reply, the father cackled incessantly like a supervillain on crack cocaine while his former fiancée and her mother broke down in a torrent of tears. The other members of the family hastily started talking about the best methods in which to dry fish to paper over the awkward emotional cracks. Glenn said it sure as hell didn't work though, the damage was done.

What struck me about Glenn, and the reasons I felt we understood each other, was that we were born into normal families with no real reason to be depressed or mentally ill, yet here we were. Alienated so much that we were forced into self-imposed exile. I mean, Glenn was forced to move by the unknown pressures of modern society not once, but twice. These were the types of people we were. More willing to endure embarrassment and humiliation than front up to the banal, silent torture of responsibility central to the pre-conceived Western adult life.

I told Glenn my theory on this whilst getting tipsy, watching and listening to trains go by. Glenn didn't smile. He just nodded slightly and stared into the distance and took another sip of his beverage.

"Boys will be toys," he uttered.

VIAROOT

*****

Before I arrived in Japan, I did a short pick and mix tour of South East Asia. I made sure I entered the land of the rising sun with hundreds of sheets of Valium and Xanax. I procured these necessities from various dilapidated pharmacies in Cambodia. They were sure to come in handy during those dreary nights in my apartment and those neon-soaked nights out.

The first time Katie and I were intimate, I was so nervous I couldn't really get hard. She didn't seem to mind, but I was incredibly concerned this may occur again and thought it probably wouldn't be tolerated a second time. So, I took matters into my own hands. I got on the super information highway and ordered some horny goat weed from China. It was expensive but was supposedly 'top quality.' I didn't stop there though. I found out about some weird hybrid pill marketed to old men. It was manufactured in the United Kingdom. It was called Viaroot. It was 'bleeding edge' according to the website. It had stellar reviews. You applied it sublingually, so the effects hit your phallic member almost instantaneously. No waiting around or taking it prior to your date when you risked walking around with a rigid hoss for a couple of hours before the actual business commenced. I was sold. I would become a Viaroot customer.

When the erection products arrived, I carefully placed them in the drawer next to my literal mounds of Benzodiazepines. Before Katie arrived at my apartment, I took two Valium, two Xanax and ate a bunch of the horny goat weed. I hid the Viaroot behind my fluorescent blue mouthwash in the small cabinet above the sink in the plasticine washroom. The bathrooms in Japanese apartments were like these totally plastic wet rooms, kind of like what you would find on an overnight ferry or something. You could just splash water around the whole room without any limitations. I always felt like I was a lab subject or an astronaut showering in them – the concept completely foreign, the design resembling a quarantine zone more than a domestic bathroom. The Viaroot would be accessed when I felt the sexual tension had suitably escalated to a point where I could excuse myself to urinate prior to commencement as a pretence to ingest the pill. I would then re-emerge to immediately launch into a mutual intercourse attack.

I cooked Spaghetti for the two of us at my apartment after we finished work. We talked about the weird ticks and sayings our students had. There was one guy in Katie's high school class who was a specialist sword collector who could only speak in fluent English if the subject of the conversation was swords. There was another guy who she described that slept for the entire class, only waking to rub his smooth pink belly exposed under the table. I told her about a student of mine who was an artist that could not stop incessantly blinking during our lessons and informed her about another one that despised people who ate coriander. When this student found an instructor who admitted to enjoying coriander, she would banish them and never book their lessons again. Like some sort of coriander-ist (or cilantro-ist depending on where you came from). I found out there were a lot of people that hated this herb in Japan – something about a genetic disposition making it taste like soap. Katie liked sharing student stories. She especially liked any mention of coriander or cilantro in classes. She would try to bring it up in every lesson, like a torturous game for the students.

Words subsided. Wine was steadily consumed. Clothes were outcast. Moist tangerine lips hovered over our glittering tongues. Katie's lip gloss sugar eyeing me like key lime pie. When the pheromones were at fever-dream level, I took the heat out of the room and excused myself to the 'quarantine zone'. I mined the Viaroot from behind the mouth wash, the silver packet glinting blue and luminous like sunken treasure. I popped a solitary pill out of the packaging. I hesitated so I could laugh silently at the pill and my situation. I placed it under my tongue and let it melt. It tasted how I imagined the acrid brake chemicals of the metropolitan trains here would taste. Like the molecular unknowns of a deep web research chemical. The stellar reviews didn't mention any side effects. Not that there would be time to re-assess if there were.

I didn't notice any discernible difference in my demeanour after the pill dissolved – I was still nervous as hell. Though the effects of the pill were obvious when I returned to the futon and recommenced the slow strawberry kiss-down where we left off.

*****

Cherry flavour burst into the hazy smile of a fire eye. Every miniscule moment erupting into pink shiny tremulous lines. Relief on not one face, but more than just mine. Bodies unearthed and untethered in the swell of an anticipated flash. Burning uncontrollable inner laughter. Clinging doubts of mental floss acceptably unclogged, any nervous disruption of flow stymied for hours. Finally, I would not lay in bed staring at the ceiling tonight. At last, with the distinct warmth of a body in my arms, I would collapse into happy-sad blown-out sleep. Torso flanked by a supplement and a

Goddess. My feelings and senses crushed in the most tender way.

ABURAMUSHI

* * * * *

I hastily moved into Katie's new apartment after a few more months of sandwich dates and laundromat collections. She and Yukio Mishima packed up their bags recently as she could no longer afford to live in the complex adjacent to Damien's lodge. Her new apartment was even smaller than the one I sourced from Damien at the beginning of the trip and it was certainly more 'Japanese'. It had Showa era artwork on the walls. It was weird to have the eyes of Japanese aristocrats observing me while I ate, got dressed, fornicated. I couldn't quite get used to it, so we ended up hanging a sheet over that wall. Katie would work during the day at a local high school and I would conduct my weird business English classes in the afternoon and evening. I would help Glenn out at the 'clinic', as we started calling it, on odd evenings and weekends. By the time I arrived back at the apartment after these commitments it was almost 10pm. We would spend the rest of the night standing out on the balcony naked drinking cheap wine, our bare skin soaking up the humid air.

One night after our shared ritual of consuming wine naked on the balcony, I walked to the kitchen sink to get a glass of water when I noticed a visitor. Its antennae gingerly groping the air, its body perfectly still as it realised the area it had unwittingly charged into was one rife with dangers. Summer in Japan meant a lot of things to a lot of people, but one of the main things it meant was that large, intelligent, and cunning cockroaches were taking over the urban apartment complexes. I stared spasmodically at the insect, willing it to return to the damp, warm crevice it surfaced from to avoid 'the shit' going down. However, it was clearly all too late for civil and amicable co-existence as Katie turned the corner into the small kitchen partition seeking a snack.

I can't adequately describe the sound, but she shrieked like an exaggerated parody of a karate master.

"Getit. Getit. Getit." She warbled in quick succession.

The previously prone and curious bug now sensing whatever rules there were for this encounter would be set aside, the sounding of the karate pastiche signalling the game had changed. Its first movements were sideways, towards the safety of the small refrigerator, its legs seemingly moving in a straight direction but its body mass driving it on a diagonal, like its shiny carapace was on the tracks of a children's toy train set. Some sort of gravitational pull leading it subconsciously to the nearest protection despite its legs wanting to continue in a straight line.

My initial approach to this newly found dilemma was an attempt to use my sheer size to herd it towards the ubiquitous area in Japanese apartments where you take your shoes off at the front door. If I was successful in forcing it to drop into the depression, the elevated step would give me enough time and protection to control the situation and perhaps make one last thrust at flicking it out the door.

This first attempt was a failure though, as it somehow scrambled under my ungraceful torso to reach the coveted safety of the refrigerator. Ordinarily, if it was up to me, that would have been that, but knowing Katie as I did, there would be no way she was sleeping with the knowledge that a cockroach was calmly residing under the fridge. Not even stealing a glance at her, I proceeded to dislodge the refrigerator from its cosy position. The previously safe environment suddenly becoming untenable for the insect. The move had the desired effect, however, the sprawling bug shot out in the opposite direction to my planned destination, its course now firmly set for the main living area.

At this alteration of the insect's internal compass, Katie very neatly jumped in the air, letting out another one of her karate pastiche calls. I plucked a nearby art magazine from the shelf as an aid to my endeavours and swung my naked body in front of the bug once more, my knees landing with a thud like the tremble of a judo takedown. The vibrations my exposed knees initiated had the anticipated result, the cockroach abruptly shifted its direction 180 degrees. As it began to head in what I would deem the 'right direction,' I tried to assist it on its way. Careful not to let it near the refrigerator again, I engaged in a series of parries, a deliberate effect similar to what it's like to try and pick something fine up with a pair of oven mitts on. The parrying of the bug guided it to the front door, transporting it without crushing its delicate body, nor letting it wriggle free to land somewhere less desirable. Pawing the surrounding air, its legs paddling insanely, I was touching the creature but not, my hands like a forcefield around it.

Once its mass unwittingly tumbled into the alcove at the door where the shoes were, I hastily tossed the mixture of trainers and heels out of the way to get a clear view of the pest. It flailed about wildly as I went about hurling the obstructive shoes down the short hall. However, it attempted to cling to one of the shoes and nearly escaped the pit as a result. This made it even more panicked, its body flipping and circling manically. At this I fell forward to deliberately place the weight of my nude body on the door, I fumbled with the lock and then toppled into the concrete passageway outside the front of the apartment. Holding a solo slipper in hand for execution purposes, I awkwardly brushed the bug into the passageway with me. I took aim and struck it firmly with the sole of the slipper. I don't know how many times I repeated this movement, crouching naked outside the apartment in the humid summer air, but when I stopped, the bug was unrecognisable from the nubile creature it resembled before. A trail of green-yellow film secreted from what was left of its smashed exoskeleton, the glossy trail shimmering under the bright passageway lights.

When I looked up, exhausted, there were two young Japanese people staring at me, somewhat surprised to see a naked hairy foreigner heaving after a battle with a cockroach. I stood up and gave a perfunctory nod to them. I slowly backed up into the open door of Katie's, our, apartment, never taking my eyes off them. Their eyes were downcast though, looking interminably at the fallen cockroach. Respect, yet understanding in their eyes – it had to be this way in the intricate concrete jungle. Turning to Katie, who viewed the scene from the safe confines of the apartment, I embraced her with my sweaty body.

"Oh my God, you got it."

"Yeah." I puffed.

We stood for some time without moving. The air was still hot. The light from the bulb above the hallway felt prickly on my skin. For some reason, the battle with the cockroach reminded me of this bird aviary I had when I was a child. In Australia, we had four parrots that lived in this aviary when I was younger. In winter, we covered the aviary with a tarp to ensure the birds didn't get too cold.

In the morning, when the sun came up, my dad and I would go and lift the tarp from the cage to signal the start of another day for the birds. Underneath the tarp there were always hundreds and hundreds of earwigs clustered together like sacs of eggs. I don't know where they came from, or where they went during the day, but they would congregate under the tarp, awaiting our arrival in the morning. We would flip the tarp off the enlarged cage, careful not to let any earwigs slip into our jackets. We would shake the tarp and kick and swing until the creatures dispersed. The earwigs were only ever gone temporarily though, overnight they would re-emerge and amalgamate into one pure earwig mass, escaping the cold with our pet birds, awaiting our arrival to shake them out in the morning. I still don't know where they came from.

"Do you remember when it ran toward the living room?" I said.

"Yeah." Katie laughed. "You were going to let it."

I didn't really know what Katie meant by this, but when she said it, I felt all the air escape from my lungs. My mind and body severely deflated by her innocuous comment. This was the first etch in my mind and I made sure I marked it down. Our relationship was going to be fleeting – like a chocolate frog left in the sun.

CONSUMER NOSTALGIA

*****

Sometimes I buy things merely due to nostalgia. I cling listlessly to vestiges of the past. As if the taste or sight of these purchased items will reignite the feelings held at a different place, in another time. Yet, at the time, back when the past was present, when I consume the goods in the original setting, I'm sure I do not feel joy, or even awareness, that this event will spark melancholic yearnings to return to such a benign memory in the future.

In the midst and throngs of living these moments, I am not in the present. My mind and body busily recalling when the previous unregistered memories occurred. When viewed in the past, they radiate and flicker with all the beauty of a tree stripped of its bark. It is these non-images that invoke an uncontrollable urge to recreate these moments.

And endless cycle like this.

Never in a state of being. Always transfixed and obsessed by an arbitrary instant of nothingness in some other region of space and time. The act of re-purchasing the product a replication of the original image. An artifact lodged at the juncture between memory and experience. The re-enactment shattering the continuum of the master copy, forever tainting it.

Immediately after the purchase is made, pangs of regret bruise the memory – something foreign warping its surface like a ripe plum squashed by its brethren in the fruit bowl, depressed into a different shape to its ideal form. A shape it will hold for a short period of time before it is altered once more, over and over, until it eventually morphs into an unrecognisable representation of the original form.

Following this simulacrum of the 'real', the memory is politely filed into the section of my brain titled: 'nostalgic experiences re-created out of compulsion with only a little joy.'

Not to be re-visited until the mind forgets this obscure attempt to find meaning in the world and subconsciously tries again. The familiar chime of the convenience store door resounding in my ears as I make my grand entrance.

NARA, JAPAN II

* * * * *

Undefined months passed. Things were getting mundane. We felt like things were crumbling. We thought that another visit to Nara, Japan might help. We thought that consuming a small amount of psilocybin scored from a German fascist we met in a bar might be a good idea. Yes, the deer and the divine mushroom spirits would release us from this perverse relationship strain.

*****

The parks in Nara, Japan have a different tension. Crisp air stimulates your muscular-skeletal system. A faint tingle felt by nervous system and bones. Not unfamiliar, or even unpleasant. Akin to pins and needles when one has been rigid too long. Like those experienced during a crucial passage of a video game – clutching the controller with intense focus, legs going limp underneath the torso's weight, numbness unnoticed until the level's spell is broken by success or failure.

Upon reaching the 'park', it becomes apparent it is several parks clustered together – affixed shapes of grass and gravel set like haphazard bathroom tiles zoomed into a 1000x perspective. Clear boundaries present, but when one zooms out to a 'normal' viewing position it's obvious the congregation represents one object as a whole. This clusterfuck of flat vegetative plains begins to materialise organically as we walk, until eventually, almost disregarded, there are no longer any buildings surrounding us. The rules of the environment's grammar have changed. Manicured shrubs and magnificent pines the new punctuation marks of the altered prefectural district's form. We stop at a large rock and glug down the warm mushroom mix from Katie's 100 Yen thermos.

"You know Marcel Proust owned a bonsai," Katie says.

Her words do not mould or dent the air like I anticipate. Nothing is shattered or broken. Perhaps the change in environmental grammar affords such vocal dialogue.

"Marcel Proust owned a bonsai? In Nara, Japan?" I say.

"No. I mean, yes, he did. But not in Nara, Japan. He looked at it every day while writing Remembrance of Things Past."

Her concentration was unperturbed by the thoughts that occupied my mind. Oblivious that if she verbalised these thoughts in the 'developed' part of town ~10 minutes ago, the impact on the space-time continuum may have been very different.

Or maybe she was aware, and as if in tacit understanding, she did not mention it because she already knows that I know this, and she knows that I know, and I know. That we both understand it is safe to proceed after her first words uttered in the 'park' tested the air. She knows that I know, and I do, know, that is.

Though I say: "I never knew he owned a bonsai."

I walk towards a large pagoda obscured by red maples and wonder how old it is.

'Slow going' I think in an endless stream of consciousness while I gaze at it arrestingly.

People walk around and through the hollow base of the structure, which seems to be made of a material much more modern than the pagoda itself. I come into close proximity of the wall and reach out to touch it. It feels cool under my hand, a certain unidentified power brewing within its core. The tittering pulse of ancient aristocrats and noblemen.

There is a boy nearby, enraptured by the structure, he stands with his family taking notes in a small, leather-bound journal. I wonder about the boy, the family, the dynamic. Is he writing about how Marcel Proust owned a bonsai in Nara, Japan? What will he do with the notes after he leaves the town at the end of the day? Will the boy review them carefully and painstakingly in the car on the drive home, or are the notes purely appearance, taken to fulfil a cumbersome school assignment, never to be looked at again, resigned to a shoebox in the wardrobe or the back of his well-organised desk drawer? Maybe the psilocybin is making me have these thoughts, I think.

"That kid is taking notes," I say nudging Katie.

"Studious."

"Studiously diligent."

The boy is still fixed in place, glancing up every so often at the walls or ceiling of the pagoda, then returning to his notebook, limitlessly compiling. I have the urge to slowly creep around to where he stands until I can eventually peer over his shoulder. I don't know what I expect to find.

It is one of life's unexpected urges.

Just an urge.

One of many I do not act upon.

His dedicated focus to the subject matter is admirable if he is indeed taking the notes he is 'meant' to be taking. Or if not, he is an extremely good actor, his parents standing by chatting inanely while the boy plays the part of enthusiastic field student. Perhaps the voyeuristic urge to view the contents of his journal surreptitiously stem from my hope that he is drawing erotically charged pictures.

Scribbles of fleshy thighs being entered by erect members in forlorn settings. Vivid compulsions to channel the blurring inside this small boy's mind.

"What do you think he is writing," I say.

"Probably notes on history."

"Notes on history?"

"Yeah... The history of the place. For like, a school assignment. Kids in my classes have to submit stuff like that all the time."

"Wouldn't their reports all be the same," I say.

"What do you mean?"

"I mean, the content, it would be the same, unless someone got one of the 'agreed' facts wrong or stumbled upon a truth that shattered the accepted history of the topic."

"Um. Hmm… I wonder."

"They should just assign one kid to each historical object for review and then when he reports back, everyone can just copy what he wrote."

"Maybe that's him."

"That's who?"

"The kid," she says gesturing to the boy busy taking notes.

"They sent him as delegate and he will report back to the whole class. That's why he is so engrossed and consumed by his notes. He doesn't want to fail."

"Failure is not an option." I say.

"Let's hope he doesn't get one of the facts incorrect or stumble upon anything that would shatter history."

I continue to look at the boy, the intense features of his hardened little face, like the stone of a peach left in the blistering Japanese Indian summer. His perfectly combed hair illuminated by the light filtering through the red maple nearby as he furiously writes.

I can only hope that he is drawing erotically charged pictures. Blurring a little inside.

Later, in the somewhat austere and outdated Nissan Micra on the way back to her apartment, Katie obediently adheres to GPS instructions as the hum of the air conditioning lulls us into a trance. The beige dashboard instruments gleam in the sun's powerful light. And all I can think is Marcel Proust owned a bonsai in Nara, Japan as cogent thought fades into blissful indifference.

COLD CUT SILENCER

* * * * *

I just got back from a trip to the bathroom, the sheets still warm from the heat of my body when she leaned over and nudged me.

“Hey.” Katie whispered.

I made a non-committal sound in reply, trying to ignore any kind of conversation. Once my mind started interacting that would be the end of any chance of sleep for the next half an hour.

I kept my eyes closed and practised breathing slow and steadily, doing my utmost to act as if I was asleep, acutely aware I was not misleading anyone. It seemed these thoughts were having a detrimental effect on my ability to re-enter a hypnagogic state in any case, the same impact as if I were participating in the conversation.

“Hey.” Katie said, a little more forcefully.

I felt her right hand lean over to tickle me under the ribs, like she did that first time we met. I involuntarily squirmed, confirming the state of my wakefulness. She was gearing up for a second offensive when I chose to play the game.

“What.” I simply uttered. My slurred words left to hang in the musty air.

“I’m hungry.” She said. “Can you make me one of those sandwiches?”

Good God. What the hell was this?

“It’s one a.m.” I said, hoping whatever this was it would pass without any further effort required on my part.

“I know.” She said. “I woke up when you were in the bathroom and thought, ‘I desperately need one of those sandwiches you make’... Can you make one?”

‘Those’ sandwiches I made were the stuff of expat legend. They were fundamentally different from the norm around here. Bread sourced from a foreign supermarket in a severely affluent neighbourhood, the only bread you could find in Japan that is not soft and sickly sweet. The preserved meat and cheese sourced from the same store, topped with grainy French mustard sent to me as a gift from my parents. I’m still surprised the jar wasn’t smashed in the international mail. It struck me that mailmen must see packages secrete a wide array of interesting substances in their line of daily duty. Pictures of non-descript postal employees tenuously holding dripping yellow envelopes aloft plagued my thoughts.

Okay. No turning back now.

I sighed deeply and then swiftly hurled my previously immobile body from beyond the confines of the comfortable bed sheets. I rushed to the fridge, which in our 1DK apartment was only a few steps away and noisily began extracting the ingredients needed to compile the sandwich.

I slapped down a few slices of preserved meat on rye, cut a few haphazard slices of cheese, rammed in the pickles and then applied a quick coat of air-flown French mustard.

'The silencer' I thought.

The sandwich that shuts people up.

I perfunctorily closed the lid on the pickles and the mustard, rewrapped the meat and cheese so they wouldn't go dry or spoil and hastily put them back in the same position in the apartment's tiny refrigerator. I cut the sandwich in half and then just as quickly as compiling the legendary beast, I silently washed the two knives I used – one for spreading and one for cutting – along with the dull blue chopping board. I placed them in the miniature drying rack that only had enough space for a bachelor's portion of dishes and returned to the main living/sleeping area only metres away.

The plate with the freshly made sandwich was deposited with a loud clunk on the low table adjacent to the bed. My anger and frustration overtly apparent in these gestures. I climbed back into bed without mentioning a word, my demonstrative actions assumed to be enough for Katie to tell that her requested sandwich was prepared. Instead of promptly rising to eat the sandwich though, muttering her thanks on the way, she simply started whimpering softly. I listened to her intermittent sniffling for a moment, wondering how a night trip to the bathroom could turn into this.

Minor things create difficulties.

Unpredictable mundane moments tear relationships apart.

"What's wrong?" I asked only as an obligation, knowing the reason, but unsure of the exact emotion that tugged at her heart.

Why did I always fail to see this happening?

Retrospectively, immediately following this tirade of violent midnight domesticity, it was patently clear that these actions would lead to trampled feelings. Yet, any logic or rational thoughts during this arbitrary chore requested at such an obscene time were non-existent. The realisation that the result of my actions was always going to end in a cold war plagued by tears only dawning upon the first sign of gentle sobbing beside me. As I contemplated this, a strong sense of foreboding welled up in me. How did I become so blind by rage when I was asked to do anyone close to me a favour? Especially given there was nothing important I was ever doing, why did I find these disruptions so intolerable, so unbearable?

I never learned from these situations. This would happen again at the next relatively reasonable request from someone I liked, maybe even loved. What could have been a minor detour always turned into a silent melee, the empty space between me mouthing "I'm sorry" and not really meaning it cleaving us in two. This would go on until eventually, one of the apologies would hit upon its mark, or it could have been a culmination of them in conjunction with the amount of time that had passed, finally equating to acceptance and a return to neutral normality.

Although I knew this dance could be circumvented by simply complying with a request, I was certain I would soon be back in this position the next time I was asked to go downstairs to get a melon from the supermarket while I was reading a book or when I was being told a boring story that I couldn't feign interest in no matter how hard I tried (which normally wasn't very hard).

Unfortunately, it's human nature to relive bad experiences. No amount of teaching can make it go away.

ACCEPTABLE ESCAPE

*****

After the sandwich exchange, things continued deteriorating, so I moved out of Katie's apartment. The day I moved in to my third apartment in Japan, I started having visions. In the visions, there was no space between each apartment. As I walked down the stairs of the complex and walked through the main foyer, the place turned into a ghost town. The ceiling was made from recycled tile. The floor wasn't cemented. Most apartments had no flooring at all. No windows, doors, or windowsills. And that was it.

As I walked through the apartment complex, I felt overwhelmed – filled with emptiness and frustration. The floor seemed to be covered in polished glittering dust. I had to lean on what little wall furniture I could get to make my way up to the new apartment – clawing at electricity metres and mail slots on the way. As I got closer to where I thought I was meant to be, I realised I had forgotten my glasses. It was strange, because I didn't even notice they were missing. My eyes were filled with so much energy, it seemed as if they were lodged too tightly in my head. Any time I moved them there was a large grating sound in my mind. I remember thinking that I had to find my glasses, just in case I chose to stay up late watching anime after I unpacked my things.

As I finished moving my things up to the apartment, I stood in the empty room and realised I had forgotten to put down the Muji storage container I was holding. All my belongings were packed in this huge Muji box and it was apparent that not even a small part of my belongings had been moved. I had to start unpacking, because soon my motivation would be gone. If I didn't finish unpacking before dark, I knew this room was where things would end for me.

In the vision, each wall of the apartment had an image emblazoned on it. Each of the images made absolutely no sense. I walked to the back of the main room to find a picture of a girl leaning on a big, blue bed. In her world, every single living thing was completely lost and gone. I could only imagine the anguish she must have felt. I'd never seen anything quite like it. Just horrible. An existence entirely consumed by walls, the worst of the city's worst, the kind of thing that almost makes you want to cry. A world that just looks like nothingness. I moved back towards the centre of the room and it felt like something visceral was erupting from my core.

The next thing I knew, my things had been unpacked and I seemed to be wearing my glasses. Yes, I was awake. Lucid and in the midst of going somewhere. A silent sea of anime pulsed on the screen of my laptop as I slowly woke up.

*****

I liked the feeling of moving into a new apartment here. I enjoyed watching the surging effects discharged from the various types of flooring as the surface was infiltrated by light. White pine, bamboo, vinyl, strange floating faux wood material – it didn't matter what quality or type. Seemingly any floor covering in a Japanese apartment would capture and reflect sunlight. This was always most spectacular in the moments before my minimal possessions had been moved in. The shadows falling softly, painting nebulous shapes across the room's grounded exterior.

There was one unspoken rule I observed during my viewing of numerous apartments in Japan – the floors were never carpeted. My belief was that the compact size of the apartments did not afford flooring material that failed to maximise the sunlight filtering through the floor-to-ceiling windows. The deadening effect carpet had on the light too much for any inhabitant to bear. The beauty of light transference and magnification lost to the harsh textured rivets.

Even once I moved my minimal possessions in, the play of light and shadow on the flooring still had a profound effect on me. I often felt unbridled awe to be able to observe the light without pretensions, a feeling I could never aspire to in a large carpeted dwelling. Years of built up baggage wedged in the carpet's coarse pile. Memories, possessions and habits from my years of unfulfilled expectations concealed under the surface. Like a cement heft permanently dragging down my trunk.

Normally partial to music, one of the first things I would do after I had 'moved in,' which meant carefully placing my meagre belongings into very specific positions in the dwelling, was to eat a prepared meal on the low table in silence. One of the few times that music was not required to block out life's many unacceptable sounds. Headphones not needed to distract me from the dawn of everyday confrontation experienced in other scenarios.

One of the only times I felt truly grateful to be born into a middle-class white family was while sitting at the eponymous low table on the first evening in a new Japanese apartment, the line of sunlight slowly shifting across the floor in front of me as twilight settled in. This was a life where I was afforded the unique opportunity of being able to travel to distant countries and automatically be accepted as someone with permission to rent small, vacant urban apartments without question. An existence where I could take my time shopping for groceries uninterrupted, musing on what I felt like eating without distraction. Amiably browsing aisles of curry powders, strange pasta sauce flavours and orbicular shaped vegetables. Having ample choice despite the fact I understood virtually nothing written on the packages or the price tags. Though irrespective of my lack of ability to speak the language, I would never starve thanks to that universal source of capitalist truth known as money and education.

After perusing the aisles at the local supermarket, returning to my temporary, comfortable abode, dusk giving way to the tidal layers of night, I would prepare a simple meal to enjoy bathed in the peculiar ambience of the high-rise apartment. Utterly alone, but surrounded by millions, all of us listening to muted sounds like those heard deep under water, I found it hard to understand that this was one of the few 'acceptable escapes' in life. To be relatively young and 'finding myself' in another country. But the rules of the game were changing, more questions were arising the older I became. The longer this 'acceptable escape' went on, the less 'acceptable' it became.

I didn't view this as just a 'phase' though. This was more. This could be a lifetime. A lifetime of foreign supermarkets and vaguely defined art exhibitions the only obligations to fulfil. But did I have the confidence to stare into the pre-accepted terminal abyss and scream into it? The ability to announce to the world in the name of detached happiness that whatever this is, whatever I experienced in these moments, should be all there is.

To declare there is no reason to exist and be okay with it.

IZAKAYA

*****

To forget about Katie and people in general, I started to research Japanese cuisine and took a deep-dive into the history of the country's hospitable establishments that served some of the most intriguing morsels. I liked the junk food. I liked the fine dining food. I liked the convenience store food. But most of all, I was interested in izakaya. Small pub-like establishments that place equal weight on serving food and drink. They range from almost dive-like, dingy hole-in-the wall establishments that have been around for decades to sleek, UFO-like cryptocurrency start-ups that have just come into fruition. I would devour books and books and blog posts and travel articles on this shit. I would try and master some common phrases so I could reach puritan status and have a 'full on' izakaya experience. I became a master of the izakaya in private. My only problem was that I was fundamentally too afraid to set foot in the establishments I had been avidly reading about. I would get close, but my trepidation and lack of self-esteem would always win out when I was within touching distance of the magical noren – my default mode network re-routing the adventurous impulse to a neighbouring McDonalds for a late-night ebi burger combo. Like everything else I did, I was completely debilitated by concerns that I would be caught in the act of making a mistake. Why attempt to do these things if you couldn't do them perfectly? I knew that I wouldn't be ridiculed for attempting to order at an izakaya in my clumsy Japanese, but I still couldn't come to terms with the eyes. So many eyes. They would be watching. And then the ears. Small ones, hairy ones, floppy ones, droopy ones... They would be there too. Listening for any kind of imperfection. The old men seated at the bar chortling at my inability to summon the words to order a beer while I perused the food menu (which I wouldn't be able to read in any case).

I kept up my research on izakaya and eventually, one night when I was almost black-out drunk, I virtually fell into one before my inner Self could regress. It was late, even for izakaya, and I ambled into this place and kind of didn't know what to do, like a pet ferret that finds itself on a concrete highway somehow. Instead of taking a seat by myself at the bar, in a stupor I wandered up directly to the only table of people still at the joint. It was one of the ramshackle archaic dives I mentioned before – the wooden interior stained and peeling from years of cigarette smoke leeching into the air. The chairs and tables wore similar scars, imperfections as numerous as the indolent women and men that frequented the place over the seasons.

There were four people at the table. They were all dressed in neutral black. A fashionable crew. They looked entirely out of place at this low-class ragtag entity. Fashion was of no importance here, the curator only cared about proffering hearty food and drink. Only one of them could speak English, broken at that, and she beckoned me to imbibe in what they were drinking.

It was hot water and imo jochu, which is like a sort of sweet potato liquor from this small island.

I was given a piping cup. The fact I was offered this refreshment and seemingly accepted without rancour gave me confidence to settle in. Despite my newfound confidence, I was ill-prepared for the English spokesperson of the group's first question.

"Do you know, toran-su-jenda?" Said my pondering assailant of the night, eyes glazed drunk mirroring mine.

"Yes, I know the word."

"We are all… toran-su." She said, extending a bird-like claw out to the rest of the black clad crew.

Bird-like got me thinking of aviaries. Which in turn got me thinking of the word 'avaricious,' which led to me thinking about greed. And then I just got paranoid as I was hit with a strange drunken realisation that I was probably making a dick out of myself and had no place here at this table. What I thought was acceptance on the surface, may have been something entirely different underneath. I was getting into the territory of masks again. The faceless and nameless I continued to encounter never leaving my thoughts for long.

"In Japan, we are invisible. Japanese law requires toran-su people to undergo medical exams and irreversible surgeries. Look at my ID."

I didn't know what I was looking for on the ID. So, I just squinted a bit, pretended I knew and nodded knowingly. I looked around the table. The others were kind of nodding too, but not very knowingly.

I decided to give them some of my best lines, some of that drunken truth serum.

"Trans people are marginalised where I come from too. They face misunderstanding. They face humiliation. They worry that someone might be aggressive towards them. I don't know what it feels like. But for me, it doesn't matter who you are or who you want to be. All that matters is that we can sit here and share this hot sweet potato drink and push against the conventions of the world."

They sat in silence for a while after this. Then the girl who could speak English translated in a hush to the others. The nods, knowingly or unknowingly, continued. I touched my cup and sipped the contents for something to do. The imo jochu was still steaming hot. Had I gone too far? What was I thinking trying to relate to this group of friends, my sozzled brain transmitting unbridled thoughts their way. I just prayed to the unholy subconscious lords that I was not using this situation to springboard into another search for validation. Did I have any right to sit here and tell them what matters? Did I have the right to tell anyone what matters? Gender is not simple. Existence is not simple.

Before I could apologise with gusto ad nauseum the food started arriving. All the wonderful odd dishes that I learned so much about. I could recite their names, knew all of them by texture and colour. Meguro tataki, agedashi tofu, motsunabe… I just let the words out. I verbalised everything as my companions looked on in shock, their thinly veiled poker faces starting to break the mould and push into smiles.

"You know Japanese food?"

"Yeah, food. I only know food." I managed. Pause. "I'm sorry if I offended with what I said before."

None of them said it was okay, that I was forgiven, that they let me off the hook because I was drunk – or, well, I hope they did in their private Japanese, but after that we ate in silence for some time. The deft hand movements of the spokesperson indicating it was fine for me to indulge my izakaya pleasure. It was all delicious, wonderful, necessary.

As we got fuller and drunker, everyone became far more relaxed and we talked about the plight of people in general more earnestly, the best we could with language as our barrier. After an hour or so, I got up to find the bathroom. When I returned everyone was gone, the bill was paid and the previously convivial table was abandoned. I was heading towards the exit when the elderly owner stopped me and handed me a small receipt with a message on it. It said: "Thanks for talking... food + drink = same" and had a smiley cat face underneath. It was signed 'Ken' and there was a Line ID next to the name.

When I got home, while the split system heating blew directly into my face at the highest fan level again, I learned that in Japan if you are trans you have to get yourself diagnosed as having a mental health condition before you can legally transition. Only then could you give birth to your 'new half,' a seemingly pejorative term used to describe transgender people in Japan. I faded to sleep with the small receipt next to my pillow, the residual taste of sweet potato liquor and cow intestines lingering as I wondered if my melancholic malaise was warranted in this world.

Escalation of Contentment

*****

The water is not running well in my bathroom today. The smell of the stagnant water confined to the pipework on this humid day symptomatic of my desire to leave the apartment and do nothing but ride escalators. Escalators in upmarket department stores, escalators in crumbling dated '80s shopping malls, escalators in cavernous metro stations. Escalators that transcend and descend where I can observe people's faces without judgement. Satisfied that I can glide by so closely to analyse their expressions. Looking for hidden signs of contentment or tedium or pain.

I brush my teeth in the kitchen sink. The bottom of the sink has collected a pool of cloudy, bronze water. The turbidity of the fluid indicative of the thousands of microscopic organisms copulating in its body. I reach out to touch the water, gently at first, then violently to observe the reaction.

The water cleaves as though there was a grain or demarcation it was destined to follow – as if it had pooled overnight purely in anticipation of this moment. My hand parting the collection of hazy aqueous solution affirms its existence. An act that renders the two of us, man and body of water, as one entity at this exact juncture of time. Inexplicably linked through this event, we both share a seemingly meaningless moment together. Yet immediately after this monumental merger, we both revert to the status quo – a feeling of utter loneliness.

MANGA KISSA II

* * * * *

It's made with a thick rice flour dough and then rolled into little balls before being dipped into the drink.

And this is how the whole thing begins.

I can almost feel your tongue enter my mouth.

You must have had the same experience.

And by the way, your maw is really quite similar to the juiciness of Doumoshi. If you'd like to know how it tastes, here's a screenshot. I can even see your own face behind my right temple. Somnambulist images making me dizzy to the punch.

You'd be really surprised how much of you I could take in to my body, even without taking your breath, like that. And the idea is to put some of this Doumoshi into my body, into us.

And that brings up a very real point, which is that once we have the Doumoshi, and we begin to do a specific type of exercise with it, then these Doumoshi particles, which are connected together, start to become very difficult for the body to assimilate.

If we are using a large amount of Doumoshi particles, we won't be able to assimilate them. Then, what we have to do is sort of create a medium so the particles can merge. Our bodies and mouths must create a medium where the particles can amalgamate and still have a profound effect on the host.

Katie: Do you mean that in addition to the specific types of Doumoshi particles, our bodies would have to be modified for each of these Doumoshi particles?

Me: It is possible, yes. If you want to make your Doumoshi particles more specific, there are other forms of Doumoshi that you can make. In particular, if you are trying to make some love, you can use the white variety.

Katie: You are correct. When my Doumoshi particles form, it is not important if they can make love or not. Only that they can be attracted to each other, and to us.

Me: I have the same problem when I make love with you and them. I should wait one more day before making love to you.

*****

I think this may have been a conversation we had while drinking Duomoshi at the manga kissa, but I'm not sure. This sequence plays behind my eyes as I stare at the blazing colours of an anime arbitrarily chosen in a pod at Kita-senpai's. I look on at the scenes that don't really mean anything, my dismal form catatonic. My stupor too unresponsive to produce a tear as I try to recall the memory of Katie's lips forming these or any other words.

SIMPLICITY AS THERAPY

* * * * *

What was best practice? In this scenario, at this hour, the 'best practice' is to walk into a random convenience store. One with public toilets, non-descript benches for perusing the magazines on offer and of course the ubiquitous smoking zone adjacent.

I enter the store as the door chimes, the automated sensor announcing the arrival of a new customer. I walk with as much purpose as I can muster to the refrigerators at the back and pluck a cold beer from the standard selection. After selecting a choice that reads 'Yebisu - Pure Malt,' a giant gold can that resembles something made in a children's arts and crafts class, I stride back toward the counter.

The clerk greets me obsequiously, his level of formality wasted on my deaf ears as he performs his mundane routine. I point to a pack of cigarettes and mutter the English name. I am asked a question I don't understand that prompts a confused nod before the clerk continues shamefully.

He scans the beer now, a sign appearing on the cash register I am directed to touch, summoning me to enter into an agreement with the store. Yes, I am overage my finger 'answers' by pressing the screen. Providing valuable, or useless, data depending on the perspective of the receiver. Everything about the convenience store is a formula, an algorithm, yet one that occurs in real time. Monitoring and responding to our desires. Ever evolving with the preferences of the geographic locale it finds itself in.

I am referred to the price by means of gentle hand gesture to the figure now present on the cash register's small screen. I pay the clerk, careful to extract the correct change for some reason. Maybe to avoid exerting the clerk further with another step in the chain, to save the clerk's need to participate any longer in this charade, this faux exchange. One party doing all the giving.

Relieved this interaction is over for the time being. I step outside into the humid air and take out a fresh Marlboro Ice Blast. Surveying the scene of the cacophony of nearby garbage bins overflowing with refuse, I notice a pile of what must be this week's left-over umbrellas sprawled across the pavement. The collection seems to be beckoning a lucky flaneur passing by, perhaps a curious office worker or taxi driver willing to select one and revive it. Just one more downpour. Validate us they silently urge. Without use we cease to be what it is we were created for.

*****

I consume more beer back at someone's apartment, languidly engaged on the seventh-floor balcony.

"What do you want to do after this?" She mutters, her words catching in her throat, like a soft-boiled egg just swallowed, the words quivering before merging back together as the phantom spherical lump slides down her oesophagus. I think I met her at a bar. I have a complete lack of awareness at present.

I look at the night sky, unable to count any of the hidden stars due to the light pollution of the city. Her head on my shoulder, of which she is probably only vaguely aware.

"After this?" I repeat.

"Yeah. After this period of your life. The Japan period."

I try to focus on one of the thousands of tiny red lights winking slowly atop the towering monoliths in the distance. The ones used to warn planes of the height of the towers or something of the sort. As hard as I try though, I cannot formulate a clear picture of this chosen beacon. When did we forget how to do this? To strain our miniature eye muscles to observe points kilometres away with absolute clarity.

I try to complete the same activity, this time with a scratch in the air conditioning unit on the balcony in the foreground. The scratch is ~10-12 centimetres from the side of my face. My attempt to take in the details of an image so close to me equally as unsuccessful as the version of the cloudy red beacon my vision conjures from the skyline. What would it feel like to be able to do this? To be an observer of images not in middle distance. To be able to process them with precision, study them at length.

Why doesn't anyone devote themselves to the study of distance anymore? Or the study of close-up double vision due to the proximity of the observer for that matter? The ability to focus on things really far away, or really close up, opposed to the all too ordinary middle distance that humans now operate on by default to combat the daily rigours of modern life.

After attempting these activities, I decide that my focus is better left where it was. Not exploring the fact that the way I see the world is built from an infinitesimal amount of tiny dots that create a larger picture, just innocently and naively ignoring the problems a different perspective creates. Long distance, close-up – such concepts were all so confusing.

Stop doing this. My life can't allow it, I think.

Simplicity as therapy, I think.

By simplifying the palette, perhaps I could get better results than just adding more perspectives, more shades of colour.

"After this. I think I will keep things simple." I manage to reply in the same vague, catatonic way as her.

She nods.

"You aren't keeping things simple now? In the Japan period?"

"No. I think I need to destroy everything I own. Everything I know. Start again."

Restore myself to the default factory mode. Forget the things I know. Try as best I can to unlearn and hope to hell I don't find something hollow when I am stripped back to the core.

We try to go to bed, but it doesn't work. Nothing works. Things are broken. I apologise. She looks at her hands, says it's okay. I hustle to leave. She stays on her bed as I see myself out. In an alcove in the shoe area, I spot a little baggie of crushed mushrooms out the corner of my pinky eye. I think I deserve a raise for tonight's trouble, so I appropriate the small bag of psilocybin on the way out. A token of my plight.

AMBIT

* * * * *

Greeted by the sound of muffled birdsong, I opened my eyes. There was a lake. Children were swinging on an old truck tyre affixed to a large tree on the banks. Each took a running start before the tyre made a wide arc over the shimmering body of water as they precedentially plunged into its depths. Laughing and guffawing in the iridescent sunlight their undefined forms were steeped in a sepia-toned haze.

Katie was next to me, but her profile seemed to blur in and out of focus. She seemed somewhat amorphous. But there was no doubt it was her. The sense, that presence, undoubtedly belonging to her.

"Where is this?"

"You mean, where are we?" She responded from somewhere far away.

"Is this still part of the park in Nara, Japan?"

"It is... And it isn't." She responded, her fashion vague as usual.

The children were now taking a break from the tyre swing to check on their propped-up fishing rods. Watching the children reel in the lines, I was reminded of when, in her apartment, in a playful mood, she often dangled a piece of yarn in front of Yukio Mishima. I recalled the yarn retracting until eventually the contact between the receding line and the physical matter underneath separated, severing the bond temporarily until the action was performed again. The reel cast, the yarn dangled. Again, and again.

"Are there any fish in that lake?"

"Ask the boys, they seem to think so."

"They seem... So awfully distant though. I don't seem to have the ability to muster enough energy to make it that far."

In fact, I found that I couldn't really move at all. I mean to say, I did feel like I was moving, but this movement was confined to the inside of my body. I could turn 360 degrees if I wanted to, but my feet remained staunchly rooted in place. It was like my soul was able to move freely within the boundaries of my nebulous physical form, but externally I was stuck in place like a pillar or statue. The blanketed birdsong continued to twinkle in the peripheries of my consciousness.

"I feel... like jelly that has almost set. The outside of my body is solid, like a rigid barrier. But inside, things are so... well, they swirl." I said sleepily.

"That only seems to happen here. They call this place an ambit, a specific form of demarcation."

"You've been here before?" I said, the sound of my voice coming from somewhere above my left temple.

"Only with you. My last."

The children were now packing up their belongings, towels and tackle boxes in hand, their formless bodies receding into the distance. I simultaneously felt her presence beside me fading, the only remains a faint outline of her tenuous body. The sun glinted off the surface of the lake as microscopic spots of light pummelled my closed eyelids. I left them shut and watched the particles excitedly expand and amalgamate into one.

*****

I re-emerge. The weight of history truly astonishing. Tranquil fields infringe on my peripheries, the glint of her luminous form impregnating and permeating my gaze, like a hypnogogic thought that occurs while lying supine, motionless, under the covers of a familiar quilt, fleeting and meandering, yet seemingly concrete and everlasting, I lose myself to the transient nature of things.

When I re-gain focus, the drowned sound of morning traffic reminds me that others exist.

TOTTORI

*****

Katie and I took a trip to Tottori to see the sand dunes. I thought maybe the setting that inspired Kobo Abe's Woman of the Dunes could save our relationship. I was wrong. We were delivered the very real truth in Tottori. There was no relationship left for us in Japan. Our love and trust for each other was to be short-lived. It was as though we had both stumbled upon a beautiful piece of art, only to discover we had been lured into a nightmare fantasy. The outline of the undulating dunes finally revealing the absence of any real connection between us.

The hotel that night in Tottori felt strange. It was like we had been summoned to a secret space. I took off my sunglasses to get to know the place better. While Katie was relaxing in the room, I found an entrance to a dark and claustrophobic hallway lined with shelves in the hotel lobby. I started walking toward the wall, when I suddenly realised something – the shelves were filled with photographs documenting the existence of Japanese men. A large number of them were men who were apparently in their sixties but still in good health. It was as I neared the wall, observing these healthy older men, I realised that Katie and I would never be on good terms again.

*****

We tried to make love in the room. Katie stared at my erect penis. I felt so pathetic. We were in the hotel room and she was wearing nothing but a T-shirt, shorts, socks and flip-flops. Well, I guess that isn't 'nothing,' it's actually a lot. I felt like a freak – I had never felt this horny before. It was like a complete meltdown. A role reversal for my phallic member from our first sexual attempt. For some reason my hands felt so tight and painful, so I kept stroking. I started to get all wet and stuffy even though I knew it ultimately meant nothing. These weren't real feelings. Just urges. Like the ones I had felt before.

"What are you, stupid?" She said.

I sat back on the sofa and looked around, not listening at all. I knew she didn't take shit. My penis was still erect in the confusion and I tried to tell her it was just my imagination, but somehow, she just kept telling me not to talk to her for fear of saying something ridiculous.

I continued trying to talk to her though, to make her understand – to make myself feel okay, but also to ask if she was okay, because she really had nothing to worry about. She was beautiful, she would find another. I didn't want her to think I was a pervert, but I was just so confused. I thought this would be our last time, I knew I wouldn't see her again. It wasn't until I started to hear what she had to say about how selfish she thought I was that I realised something was incredibly wrong with me. She got very upset and started crying.

I tried to accept it at first, but I just couldn't. It was like she was talking directly into my brain. I started to go limp and wanted nothing more than for her voice to stop. I desperately wanted to walk away from her and dive headlong into something else. The situation was spiralling out of control.

I thought 'you shouldn't be talking to me like that' and numerous other similar things, but I couldn't verbalise any of them. Just when I was about to leave the room, I felt her hand close around me and gently press down. Maybe there would be a last time. It didn't hurt like the drill that I'd felt before with her during these sensual moments. She didn't make eye contact and never said anything. Afterwards, all I could think about was how stupid it was to make her feel this way, how stupid it was to allow myself to get caught in this trap. I started crying as I stood there completely stunned. Her gaze lingered on the side of my head, but what I could see was just her hand caressing the back of my hand where there was a scab healing. Her eyes focusing down on the plush carpet at her feet.

"I'm done." I said, my eyes meeting the downlights embedded in the ceiling, my voice as cold as snow that no doubt had dried over the years. It didn't matter though, she didn't hear a word. She had already left.

*****

I woke up the next morning with a new wound and a new-fangled pain. The only thing that was left was the cold truth and I had to sit directly in front of it. I sat up quickly, knuckled my eyes, then looked down at my hand, which had dried blood on it from the scab. I stared blankly for a while before I knew Katie was gone and realised I had fallen asleep.

"What the hell are you..." I said without thinking.

My hand started to shake, the aches and pains starting to set in.

As much as I wanted to get up and kick at the walls, there wasn't enough essence left in me to do it. So, I put on my best mask and pretended I was talking to myself. I remembered the last moments with Katie in Tottori and the faint smile that moved around her profile like a cursor on her face. Those dunes were never going to be enough to save us. Like Kobo Abe, my loneliness too was an unsatisfied thirst for illusion.

MODERN DAY TRAVEL

*****

I immediately took another trip to the coast to escape my wicked demons. Those underlying pitiful feelings left for Katie and all the rest. The first thing you notice about beaches in Japan is that they are empty. Zones without time. A place that could be anywhere if not for the lack of vegetation and anything remotely man-made. The beach I visited was the same image of those seen hundreds of times before during my childhood back home, but as if someone had deftly and precisely erased any surrounding foliage and structures leaving the unblemished sand, water and cobalt blue sky intact. If it was a recording, stereo sound would not be available. A mono-coastal setting experienced without optional accessories. Shocking in its minimalist form.

While attempting to grill scallops on a tabletop barbecue in a concrete seaside shack, I could barely turn away from the barren scenery outside. A dim haze present while I tried to figure out what icons normally filled the vast gaps in space that confronted me. After eating my portion of market price bivalves and soft-bodied invertebrates, I unceremoniously left the sparse seaside environs without even setting foot on the infinite plains of yellow sand. An unspoken agreement between my Self and I that going any closer would be too much to bear.

*****

On the way home, I keep myself going by reciting the list of things I am going to do when I get back. This is how I deal with travel. I don't dislike this feeling. I wouldn't want to experience it every day, but I don't think it would be the same feeling if it was experienced that often. It would cease to be the same experience, it would be defined as 'something else.'

The mental list of things is this:

- Glass of water
- Toilet
- Shower
- Food
- Sex
- Sleep

Basic urges. Basic requirements. Things that are too difficult to do holding so much luggage. Things that are far more enjoyable at an end point, in private.

The joys of cool liquid cascading down my throat, the ecstasy of hot water from a showerhead cleaning my sweat-ridden body, the comforts of taking my time on the toilet. Knowing the only place I need to be following this moment is the next item identified on the mental list.

I seldom stood up when I went to the toilet anymore, I much preferred sitting down regardless of what I needed to do. It was more relaxing this way. Why were men in such a rush? We were no longer hunter gatherers, there was no danger of a lurking beast in the shadows preparing to snatch our bodies so why did we need to remain so alert? Animal instincts had been eliminated.

It was the same with eating. The preparation of even the simplest meals should take time. This is especially true after reaching the terminus following travel. Take for instance a tuna salad sandwich. First, you get the two pieces of bread out and place them on a chopping board. Gather all the ingredients from the fridge. Lather one piece of bread with mayonnaise, the other with mustard (French of course). Take out two tiny Roma tomatoes and cut them into ~4 pieces. Lightly sprinkle salt and pepper on them. Tear off a small amount of lettuce, wash this portion alone and shake dry. Slice this into manageable pieces. Extract a pickle from the bunch submerged in brine, cut that into pieces too. Open the can of tuna, carefully remove 4-6 pieces of flesh from the can and place them on the bread. Rye, of course. Evenly space the tomato segments and pickle pieces on top of the fish. Scatter the lettuce over that. Place the other piece of bread on top and push down firmly, but not too forcefully. Use a different knife to cut the sandwich in half – a serrated one. The one used to spread the condiments won't do. Settle the sandwich halves on a plate. Cover the remaining tuna and shuttle the ingredients back to the confines of the refrigerator. Wash the chopping board and knives. Wipe down the kitchen bench. Sit down in silence to eat the crafted sandwich, slowly. Accompany with a glass of water to force it down your parched, raw tongue and throat the aeroplane air has stripped bare.

Modern day travel, the Great Creator.

*****

After eating, I brush my teeth. I am wearing baggy cotton pants with no underwear and a comfortable T-shirt. I lean into the mirror to examine my profile, determine the evidence of temporary damage by the Great Creator. Know that time and sleep will erase these features. Know from experience.

Shuffle gently from the bathroom to the bed. There is a strange sensation on my skin, on my hair. Draw the curtains, slip into the covers, close my eyes. And wait for sleep to come again.

HEART IS HARD OF HEARING

* * * * *

Walking through windswept streets. Images of neon lights in the rain. The moon is bright, the night is dark, and on and on and on. Who was it who said sometimes all we have is clichés? Sometimes all we have is clichés and the earth feels like it is gasping for air. How did we fade into this world? An orb of fish out of water clichés. A race of highly intelligent beings that reached their apex only to entirely displace themselves from the ecosystem they created. Now we wander around, like round pegs trying to be smashed into square holes, hoping, craving that we fit in somewhere else. Words and explanations often make me want to scream. They make me want to scream in silence.

As I walk past dessert shops, laundromats and small izakaya's – the decorations of a common Japanese thoroughfare all now so familiar, I try to reignite my previous vigour, try so hard to emulate my prior feelings when traversing these streets months ago. But no matter what I try – listening to the same songs, recalling 'fond' moments, closing my eyes and trying to melt into my former Self – the feelings just won't come. They cannot be replicated. My heart has lost its ability to hear, the ability to listen and respond to the same stimuli in an ethereal manner now this setting is no longer alien. All freshness and excitement eclipsed in seamless evaporation.

I climb a set of steps onto a pedestrian overpass and opposed to continuing to cross then descending the steps on the other side, as its construction intended, I simply stand in the middle of it, staring into the forceful wind, gazing at the infrequent lights of commuting taxis and squat minivans below. I sip my mega-can of Asahi and desperately try to recall Katie's face. Initially, it is just a vacant space filled with the faces of movie stars my brain thinks closely resemble her, but eventually, these rows of Doppelgangers coalesce into a more accurate depiction of her profile. When I have formed the memory as best as possible, I reach down into that deaf cardiac pit and attempt to feel something. It is hard. It feels forced. As much as I try though I realise something – I am not a memory maker. I'm just a person.

My journey moves on after this abject failure as I cross the overpass. I decide in these forlorn times, perhaps a browse of the products at the nearest convenience store will revive me. The quaint foreignness of these institutions has generally been able to resuscitate my stuttering body in the past. I enter the store and realise I recognise the song playing over the speakers and it instantaneously makes me ill. I browse the shelves for a product I have not seen before but all I can see is banal familiarity. I begin to panic. I turn on my autopilot. Cruise on default. Quickly grab a can of beer and ask the clerk for one of the lonely kaarage chicken sticks that remain in the warmer by the counter. There are two pathetic, tepid sticks left. When the clerk extracts the one I request, it feels like plucking a kitten out of the litter from a pet store to take home, leaving the others vulnerable and confused. It feels truly awful. I am breathing heavily now. I nearly forget my change and fumble out the door. The fish out of water cliché is prodding the peripheries of my consciousness. Repeat mantra: sometimes all we have is clichés.

I regain control after sitting on a bench, motionless for several moments, and begin to walk in the general direction of my third rented apartment, most stores and restaurants now closed. The only light left of the night emitted from the odd row of vending machines huddled together every few hundred metres. Gentle hues of white and blue reflected in puddles of water. I stare at my kaarage as I walk, watching as its form is intermittently bathed in vending machine light. After I eventually eat the chicken stick, I have nowhere to look but the ground on which I walk. The shape of things to come expressed in the form of hollow pools.

COMPLEX ROOM

* * * * *

Crescents etched into faces.
Shapes burnt into eyes.
Manifest distant tremulous lines.
Hard enough strain to create a hole.
Remember that it is all done to show your power.
It seems I have created a new form of man.

The walls of these rooms contain more than enough material to build a complex society. I have only a very limited amount of information as to what it is that I am doing – is this life? If something does happen, I want to know. I just need an opportunity to find out. I will find somewhere I can go back to. Even if I don't remember where. If a memory of someone does come up, I will remember.

HALLOWEEN

*****

We ride our bicycles up to the condensed façade of the Don Quijote north of the river, the building squished like a jpeg image altered to fit a Powerpoint slide. We both dismount at the bicycle rack adjacent – me on my silver fold-up companion, Glenn on his huge, green mountain bike. It is a visual monstrosity when parked next to my gleaming, compact ride. It looks longingly, hungrily, like a predatory praying mantis. No doubt his machine wins when it comes to cunning and speed, but mine easily accounts for 'big green' in the all-important department of aesthetics. I love my bicycle. So much so that I have christened her with a name: Hitomi-chan. To me, she represents the irresistible quirkiness of so many young Japanese girls. She represents the dependability and reliability of a dutiful spouse. She is equal parts fashionable and practical. She is the image of enlightenment in the age of anonymous supermarket browsing. We have been through a lot together.

It is Halloween. Halloween is popular in Japan. It appeals to the masses here on a surface level. People enjoy that you do not have to think too deeply about the underlining reasons of the event. That they don't have to take it, or themselves, so seriously. It is a known fact that people in Japan take their lives 98.56% seriously. It is nice to have a break from this pressure. It must be wonderful to forget the strain of previous generations sitting on your chest, crushing your soul with honorific suffixes, even for just one night while you dress up as a sexy vampire or a cute werewolf or a brooding black widow (whatever that is).

We have come to the nearest Donki mega-store in search of supplies. Our job is to 'haunt' the classrooms, to frighten Japanese kids with the blinding intensity of mass-produced decorations. Glenn is freaking out. He has searched everywhere in the nation of Japan for black garbage bags and his search has yielded none. He says they must be black. All light must be obfuscated. All walls must be covered. The children must have the correct atmosphere to shit themselves with candy-induced excitement and fear. Glenn tells me that the supermarkets, the convenience stores, the hardware stores, the cleaning supply stores, the online stores only deal in translucent or white garbage bags now.

"There was a law change," he mutters to himself, his mind appearing frazzled like one of the schizoid box men we see under the bridges, financially crippled and mentally broken.

"I'll have to make some phone calls," he says to nothing but humidified department store air as he looks in the direction of a towering golden pyramid of skin cleanser bottles.

Despite what Glenn says, we find black garbage bags with relative ease. When we find them, Glenn does not act surprised. He just scrutinises the package, his face vibrating slightly like a miniature sun is desperately trying to escape his mouth, straining almost tearfully as he reads the hieroglyphic text emblazoned on the waxy surface. After what feels like several minutes, but probably more like ~45 seconds, Glenn snaps out of his reverie, scooping up the remaining five packages of black garbage bags and piling them into our basket.

"Yes, these will work," he affirms, eyes glazing over like a shark during a feeding frenzy.

We buy the black garbage bags, a stack of Jack-O-Lantern cut-outs, some weird shit that looks like charcoal fairy floss.

"Mist... Or spider webs... Maybe." Glenn explains regarding the fluffy stuff.

I pocket a set of vampire fangs with artificial blood capsules on the way to the registers. I am not planning to dress as a vampire, but for some reason I feel these moulded bits of plastic and capsules of food dye are worth stealing. Worth getting caught and fumbling an explanation. Worth deportation. Maybe I can give them to one of the students and make them smile. Make them think fondly of me in ten year's time when they have stable employment as a banker or real estate salesman. If I leave little memories in people here and there, perhaps I won't be ceremoniously forgotten. My life here is full of subconscious gestures that seek to validate my existence, to avoid my body being exhumed as just another foreign ghost. I want someone, anyone, to have a memory of me that is ineffable. Yes, the exhilaration of shop-lifting these fangs must be the answer to my woes.

Glenn awkwardly pays for our swag by skimming the contents of his wallet, ensuring he purges it from as much small change as possible. It's uncomfortable for all concerned, but he has to do it. He is forced to do it by some unknown blockage that resides within. I understand why. I have the same unavoidable compulsions. This is why Glenn and I get along, we both have no 'real' excuses not to be healthy functioning members of society, but we are crippled by something indescribable. Fucked by mild swells of OCD and paranoia over nothing substantial. No history of drug addictions, no background of family trauma, no unwanted sexual abuse. Just a shared curtain of banal middle class, white suburbia – one in the southern hemisphere, one in the northern. Childhoods full of mowed lawns, all-important sporting events and lectures on the importance of responsibility.

I once was on Skype with a friend from back home and I told him I was living in a small apartment here in Japan. That it was essentially one large room with a futon, a low table and chair, a balcony and an alcove area where the kitchen, shower and bathroom were located, which was also basically the entrance. I told him how much I enjoyed it. How I didn't have to waste time cleaning, or maintaining useless possessions, or attempting to fix 'odds and ends' around the place. No hardware, no gardening shit, no tool shed – my maintenance life now consisted of a pack of wet wipes and a dustpan. He responded by saying that it sounded great, but what would I do without a lawn to mow? I wished sarcasm was present, but the dead air while he awaited my sincere response made it evident that it wasn't. Mentioning these little nuggets on why I felt compelled to leave the 'lucky' life, most people just looked at me blankly. They didn't understand the forces that drove me into exile. Only rare individuals like Glenn understood. He didn't have to say it, but his actions were befitting of a person that simply didn't fit in – a person exactly like me. We were people with only two options: to comply to the rules of expectation and live a painful existence while screaming in silence every night or get up, say an emotionless good bye and leave. At least then our parents had the option of saying "Look at my child, he is travelling the world" while not forcing them to admit their offspring was an abject failure in the all-important eyes of cultural norms. No marriage, no mortgage, no kids, no responsibility, no respect. At least exile gave everyone involved with people like Glenn and I the image of a tiny bit of respect. Not that any of these pathetic shreds of the word were real in any way.

*****

In the classroom, we are stapling the garbage bags to the walls. I have the fangs in my pocket. No one is the wiser. Glenn is 'double-bagging' the windows. He really doesn't want any light seeping in. He doesn't want the kids feeding off the real world. He craves immersion. He feels they deserve this. I am constructing a cardboard box maze/tunnel-like structure for the kids to crawl through. I am hanging the fluffy charcoal fairy floss shit from the makeshift roof of the structure at random intervals. It feels nice. The process of decking out the room make Glenn and I act like we are alive. Like we are human after all. When we feel the job is respectable and basically complete, we each crack a giant can of Asahi to celebrate. As we take a swig from the delicious amber fluid, Glenn almost gags, bits of foamy beer escape from the sides of his undulating lips and run onto his crinkled green overshirt. He coughs and gasps, eyes wild with apprehension.

"Egh, we forgot the music." He blurts. "The fucking Halloween playlist. The eerie… The eerie… Eerie fucking music."

I look at Glenn and ask if we can use last year's playlist, if he knows where it is.

"Negative," he says.

I am tired. I don't want to do anymore work on this. The feeling of being alive dissipating as I realise that Glenn won't let this go. The kids must have accompanying music. To Glenn, this is a deep burger without fries situation.

I eyeball Glenn. Tell him to calm the fuck down. Tell him that we are slamming down our beers and riding to Bookoff. It will be okay, I say. We will find something that fits our theme there. The haunting will be complete. It will be miraculous. It will be memorable. It will be ineffable. This 'pep' talk focuses Glenn somewhat and we automatically finish our beers in silence under the harsh fluorescent light of the education centre's front office.

The ride to Bookoff is smooth. Hitomi-chan struggles to keep pace with Glenn's flying mantis. I love that all around me there are flashing lights, concrete structures and billboards, but virtually no sound. Japanese cities have a peculiar way of doing this. Even the rampant markers of ever-increasing consumerism are respectful of the night air. This same air mollifies my skin, percolates my blood. I start to feel life coursing through me again.

Glenn is what some would term an experimental music aficionado. Undoubtedly lumped into the category of psychedelic rock otaku. His tiny apartment, which is even smaller than mine, is full of obscure records from vintage shops in Japan or shipped in from strange places like Cologne or Plzen or Novosibirsk. The same Glenn who doesn't even have a bed, who counts out his small change to buy the cheapest curry rice on the menu at Sukiya, spends literally thousands of dollars a year on records. He is not 'normal'. But it's okay, I don't judge. Like I said, I am aware, I'm far from 'normal' either.

At Bookoff, a second-hand store full of books, DVDs, CDs and other shit that are pre-packaged as if new, Glenn takes an astounding amount of time sifting through the CDs to see what might fit our requirements. Everyone browses Bookoff for hours. It is expected. It is why it is a successful chain. Teenage kids can consume an entire manga series in the confines of these stores without losing any hard-earned Yen. The people at head office don't give a fuck. The people at head office are masters of encouragement. As long as the orange and black logo is subliminally tattooed to the interior of the browser's brain, they will eventually consume something so undeniable they have to make a purchase. Head office know what they are doing.

Glenn has found an album by German Krautrock band Can he has intimate knowledge of. He is confident it will create the right atmosphere to scare the kids rigid. The album is ridiculously expensive. I tell him with words from the wall that I can't afford to pay that.

"Write off," he mumbles. "All good, all good. It's a write off," he keeps muttering on the way to the register.

This is his way of saying that the freshly purchased disk will form part of his burgeoning collection. I am relieved from any form of monetary contribution.

*****

We listen to the album's seven tracks in their entirety in the haunted room. The uncanny psychedelic notes cascade in the space enclosed by black garbage bags. The space we have created. We don't say much, just sip some more on our eponymous giant cans of Asahi. It feels like these carbonated cans of goodness have taken over our souls here in Japan. The opalescent chrome logo of the iconic beverage has fully and radically replaced our names. We have been reduced to mere punctuation, the cans and cans and cans of beer have become the body of our work. The substantive content. As Glenn and I breathe everything in, I gently shut my eyes and contemplate what I would most like to be in the room. The charcoal fairy floss stuff, the deformed notes of Michael Karoli's Olympic White Fender Stratocaster, the light trying to force its way through the layer of black garbage bags? I decide I would really like to be a bubble in the amber liquid of one of our Asahi's – to be full of agitated, yet graceful excitement, nervous with energy as I float to the top of an aqueous body of liquid, fleeting in my existence as I climax into a beautiful, delicate plop. When I open my eyes, Glenn is jiggering his knee and playing air drums to the music, humming to himself with a slightly deranged look. I lean over and closely examine the non-descript black running shoes I have on. Confused, I take out the plastic vampire fangs and blood capsules. I turn them over in my hands as it becomes apparent that I am still myself.

FORTUNE II

*****

I am rummaging through my Muji drawers. I'm on the search for my master find. That beautiful bag of dried mushrooms I snatched from the girl's house where my soul fragmented and broke. It's been a while since I have felt something. It's time to give the journey around my skull another try. Mea Iter Skull. I don't know if that's Latin or just something I made up. Nothing matters at this moment but ingesting these crushed carriers of 4-HO-DMT. I don't have any lessons booked at Dainichi tomorrow. I don't have any kids to manage at the afterhours 'care' centre with Glenn. I don't have any lovers or likers or haters left, like Katie, no one that needs to be considered or concerned. Just an appropriate void in my calendar that needs to be filled with serotonergic wonder and glee.

I mix the contents of the furrowed bag into an old sake vessel combined with Ginkgo Biloba tea, both cup and tea parting gifts from one of my affluent students down at the pleasure parlour when he moved town. I blow a head of steam over the receptacle cradled in my two feathery hands. I watch the sunlight move across the faux white pine floor as I sip, lap and gulp the acrid innards. I ingest the brackish volume any way I can. I lie supine on the hard floor as moments of benign mental traffic and anxiety give way to curved light, like a stone wall crumbling, inches of profoundness manifesting in the apartment's curved lines. Mottled pinks and greys in the body of the rustic cannister begin to bloom. Streaks of colour bleed out of its foreign matter. Rivulets of Appalachian ingress radiate like rose quartz in my eyes. Neuroplasticity. Higher energy realm. This is my ascension, now.

I'm in Queen Himiko's tomb, I think. The street shaman I encountered that drunken night is here too. Her crooked smile beaming, her shadow drapes over me like an abject celestial fiend. Even upon our first meeting, inebriated on the Queen's juice, I somehow knew she would be the harbinger of my inner vision. My foreign angel dripping in chromakey nebula. Her presence perfectly timed in my penultimate routine simulation. The street shaman asks me if I want to dance. She tells me what I have consumed is 'dance-inducing.'

"Odoritake!" her voice keeps reverberating above my right temple. "Odoritake!"

My mind eddies, whirls, flashes and settles on an image of Katie and I in the summer. We are eating ice cream at a shrine. I try to re-enact something from a TV show to impress her, make her laugh, wild hand movements causing my freshly made black sesame ice cream to fall on the grass. The juxtaposition of the charcoal slurry against the bright green grass is jarring. The image is as vivid as reality. I feel incredibly disappointed. I touch the outline of my shame. Katie tells me that whenever she drops an ice cream, or feels stupid and sad, all you have to do to feel better is create a little dance. She does a little dance. It is fluid. It is liquid. She is unequivocally beautiful in this moment – then, here and now. I try to reach out and caress her form, but I merely slip through a perimeter that resembles melted plasticine. I fall through this translucent funnel, as microscopic bubbles fizz past my line of sight. At the bottom of the funnel, it is dark. She is gone. I am back in the ancient Shamaness's tomb.

My body is lying on a big pile of dirt. I am sinking into an earthen aperture. A giant key is extracted from the pocket of the street shaman's cloak. It is pressed down on my mirage, heating and searing my remains. I am covered in a barren mound of clay. My essence floats around me on deaf air. The street shaman whispers to my amygdala in the darkness. Her message to me audially clear.

When my mind clears enough to regain control of my faculties, I am kind of half-sitting, half-lying on my futon. I have my bright orange notepad open besides me. There are a bunch of scrawls and squiggly lines drawn. Buried in amongst the hieroglyphs, there is one clear sentence that can be read though.

It simply says: 'Break the glass and twinkle the bell.'

XMAS

* * * * *

I stood on the subterranean platform (again). I watched advertisements transmitted on screens (again). Every now and then, I was overwhelmed by people. By their living breathing faces as they rushed past. I was in shock that these people grew from children. That they could walk around. That they had brains. Just like me. I couldn't believe I was one of them and that's how I must look. Despite the mild weather, my insides were melting. The gloopy concentration unnervingly crushed.

One voice spoke from inside: "You're supposed to be a hero, but you just can't be. All it would take to make you a real hero is a drop of blood in the wrong place. But you're an artificial rooster, a cock with no crow."

An image flashed through my mind of an enormous, shining metal ball suspended in the air. I saw myself, the one who would be an ideal avatar, my soul the materialised reality. My body was growing smaller. I felt as if the planet could begin to unravel from me. As the train doors opened, a familiar jingle played. At this point I was truly cognizant that I wouldn't live forever. One day, I was going to die. Something had to change, something needed to change. I had to be brought back to life. I had to be able to see and hear (again).

It was Christmas, but I didn't care. I was too busy getting the metro train back from the supermarket. I was in the business of celebrating alone. I was planning to cook teriyaki salmon in the weird fish broiler they have in Japanese stoves. Kind of like a flat oven, but it sort of toasts the contents until the flesh pops brown and gold. When I arrived at my apartment, there was an air mail package from my mother. I opened it up. The contents were a scarf and a new jar of French mustard. There was no card. I put on the scarf without taking the tag off. I stared at the jar of mustard until my eyes hurt. Where was the card?

*****

Shogeki.

I carry the mustard outside into the apartment complex hallway. The hallway light glints off the glass jar. It eats my eyes with tiny minerals. I pick a door at random and knock on the chosen neighbour's door. A dishevelled old man comes to the entrance. His body is bent. He casts me an apprehensive globe. I thrust out the jar.

"Merry Christmas." I say.

The mustard is yours.

He takes the gesture in, slightly amused, and shifts the jar's weight with a deft turn of his palm. He performs the glance of a flamingo. His oily vitellus breaks into a smile. Facial features still buried, he manages to bow, if only to be polite. In possession of a curious caterpillar on his upper lip, the muscles quiver in anticipation of a word. He turns to go inside, but no sound escapes his mouth. The jar of mustard held close in his damp hands. Submissive to its new

God.

I stand prone as the door clicks shut. The scarf feels itchy around my neck, but I don't take it off. I wrap it around a little tighter and look down the awning corridor. My body involuntarily trembles under the glare of the hallway lights.

Here I am.

Dale Brett is a writer and artist from Melbourne, Australia. He is interested in exploring the melancholic malaise and technological ennui of the 21st century. Faceless in Nippon is his first novel. Banal artifacts of an absurd reality found @_blackzodiac.